JONATHAN SWIFT'S

GULLIVER'S TRAVELS

A GRAPHIC NOVEL

BY DONALD LEMKE &
CYNTHIA MARTIN

STONE ARCH BOOKS
A CAPSTONE IMPRINT

Graphic Revolve is published by Stone Arch Books
A Capstone Imprint
1710 Roe Crest Drive, North Mankato, Minnesota 56003
www.capstonepub.com

Cataloging-in-Publication Data is available at the Library
of Congress website.
Hardcover ISBN: 978-1-4965-0014-4
Paperback ISBN: 978-1-4965-0033-5

Summary: Lemuel Gulliver always dreamed of sailing
across the seas, but he never could have imagined
the places his travels would take him. On the island of
Lilliput, he is captured by tiny creatures no more than
six inches tall. In a country of Blefuscu, he is nearly
squashed by an army of giants. His adventures could be
the greatest tales ever told, if he survives long enough to
tell them.

Common Core back matter written by Dr. Katie Monnin.

Color by Benny Fuentes.

Designer: Bob Lentz
Assistant Designer: Peggie Carley
Editor: Donald Lemke
Assistant Editor: Sean Tulien
Creative Director: Heather Kindseth
Editorial Director: Michael Dahl
Publisher: Ashley C. Andersen Zantop

Printed in the United States of America in
Stevens Point, Wisconsin.
052014   008092WZF14

TABLE OF CONTENTS

ABOUT JONATHAN SWIFT

Jonathan Swift was born on November 30, 1667, in Dublin, Ireland. His father had died several months earlier, and his mother decided Swift should be raised by relatives. Swift's mother gave baby Jonathan over to Godwin Swift, her late husband's brother. Godwin, an attorney, enrolled Jonathan in a prestigious school, which fostered Swift's love of reading and writing.

In 1682, Swift graduated from Trinity College in Dublin, which was one of the most respected colleges in Europe. He then traveled to England with dreams of becoming an important church member. He soon returned to Ireland, however, to continue his education. He eventually became the dean of St. Patrick's Cathedral.

Despite living a busy life, Swift never lost his love of writing. Over the years, he wrote several books (some of which were published under a pseudonym, or pen name) and earned a reputation as a talented satirist.

In 1726, he published *Gulliver's Travels*, a story that is still popular to this day.

GLUMDALCLITCH

LEMUEL GULLIVER

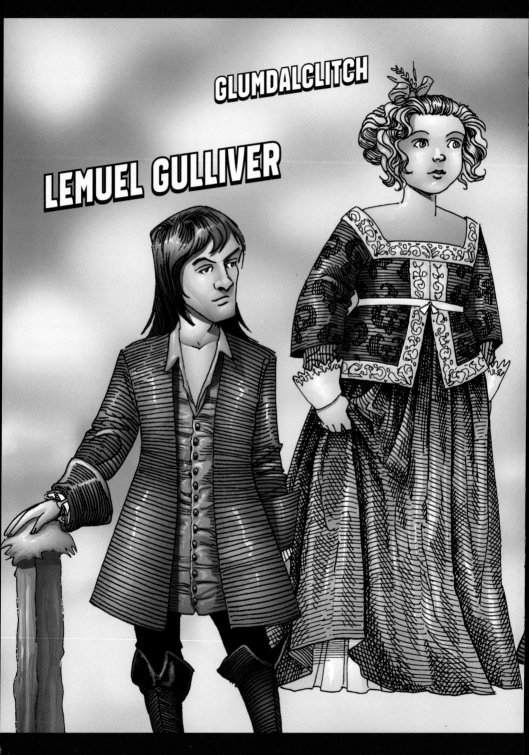

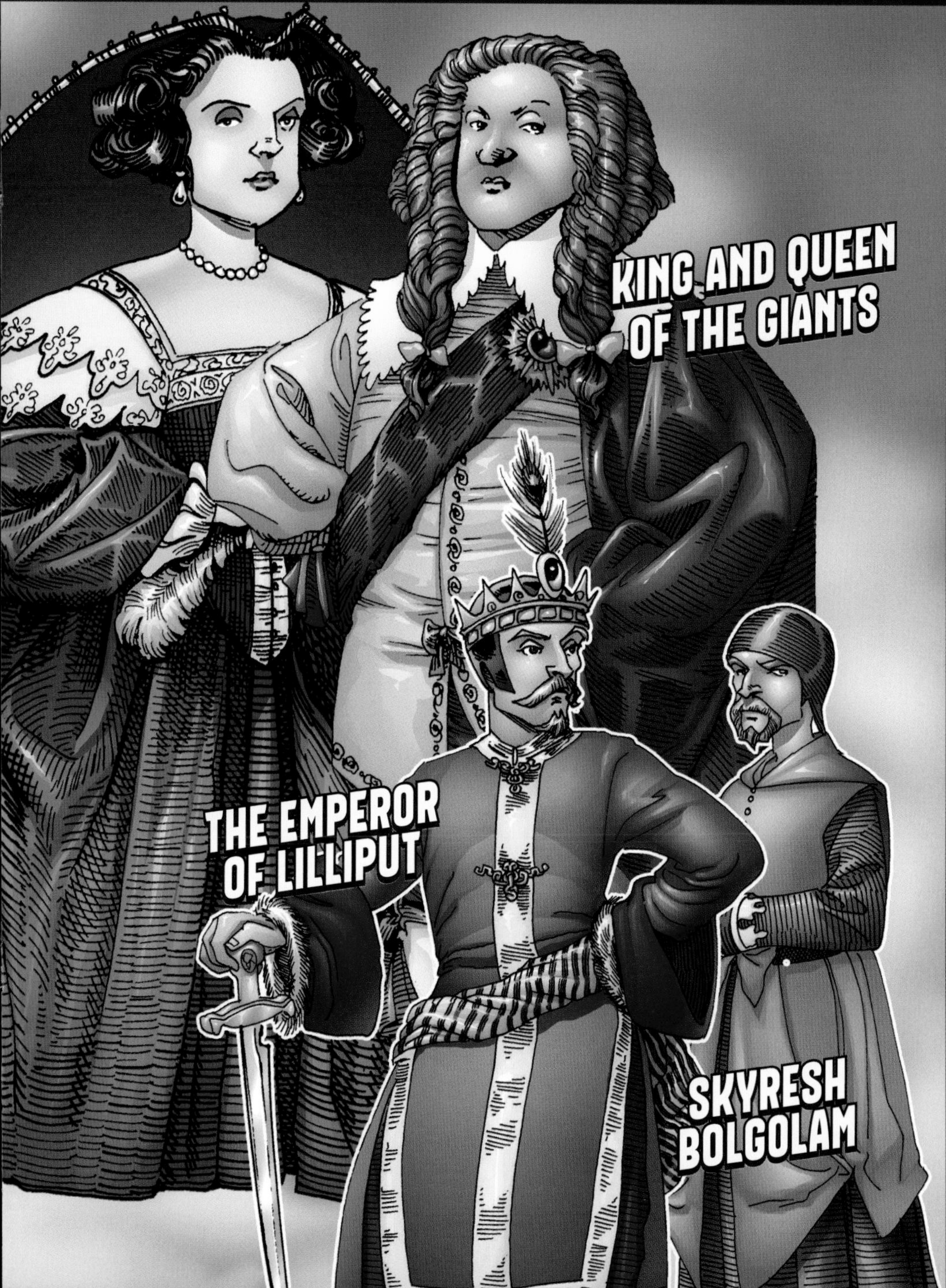
KING AND QUEEN OF THE GIANTS
THE EMPEROR OF LILLIPUT
SKYRESH BOLGOLAM

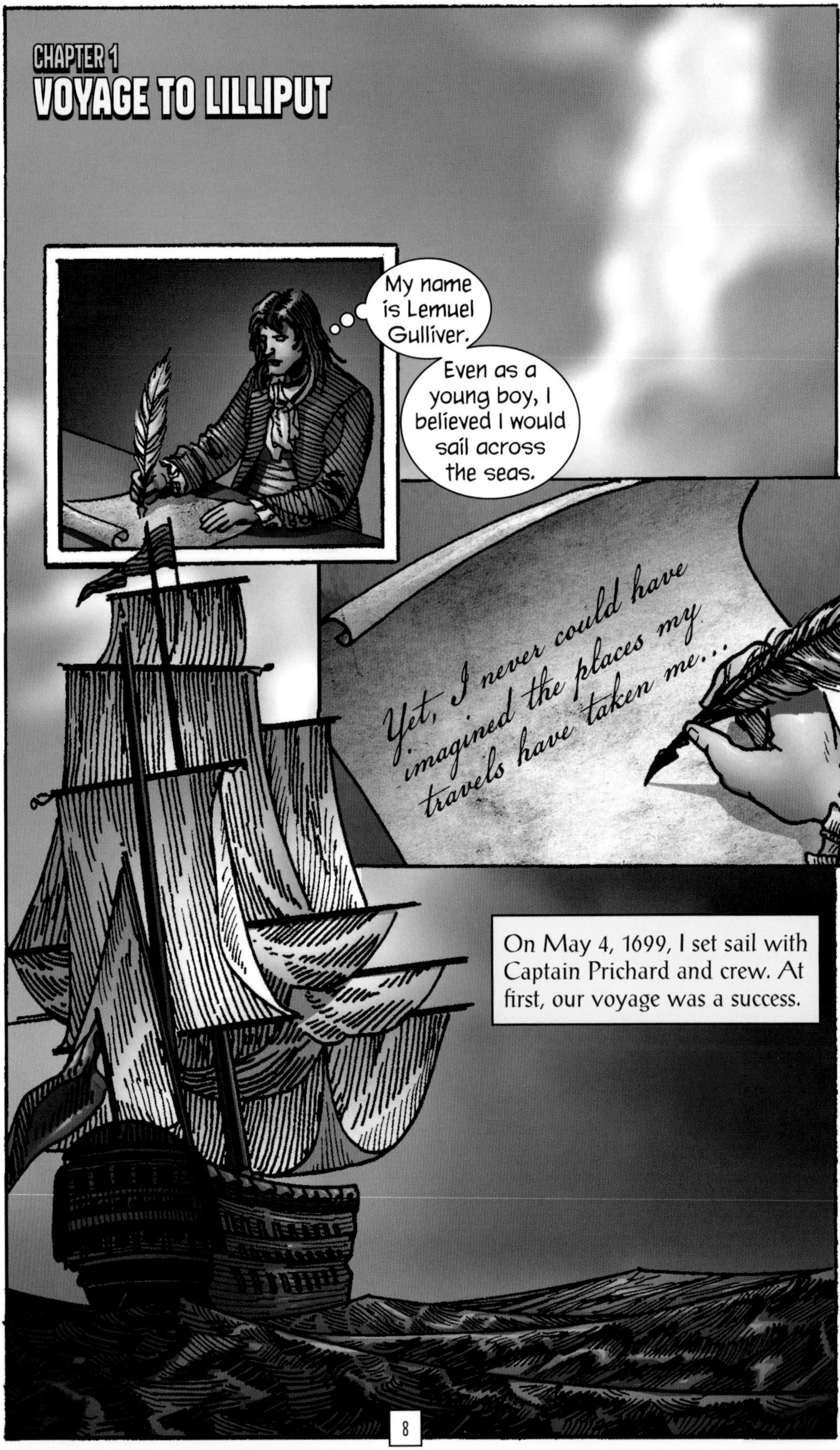
CHAPTER 1
VOYAGE TO LILLIPUT
My name is Lemuel Gulliver.
Even as a young boy, I believed I would sail across the seas.
Yet, I never could have imagined the places my travels have taken me...
On May 4, 1699, I set sail with Captain Prichard and crew. At first, our voyage was a success.

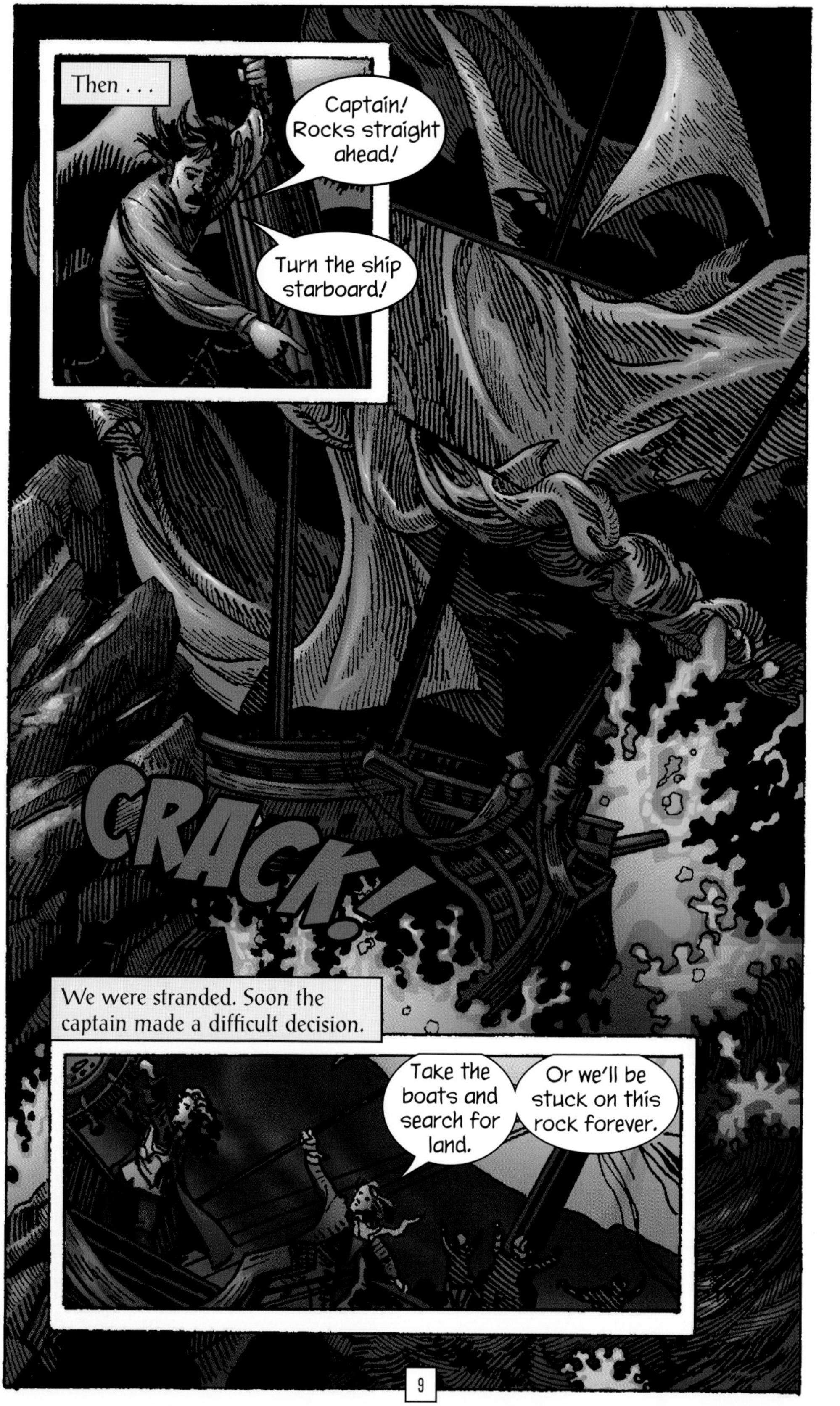
Then . . .
Captain! Rocks straight ahead!
Turn the ship starboard!
CRACK!
We were stranded. Soon the captain made a difficult decision.
Take the boats and search for land.
Or we'll be stuck on this rock forever.

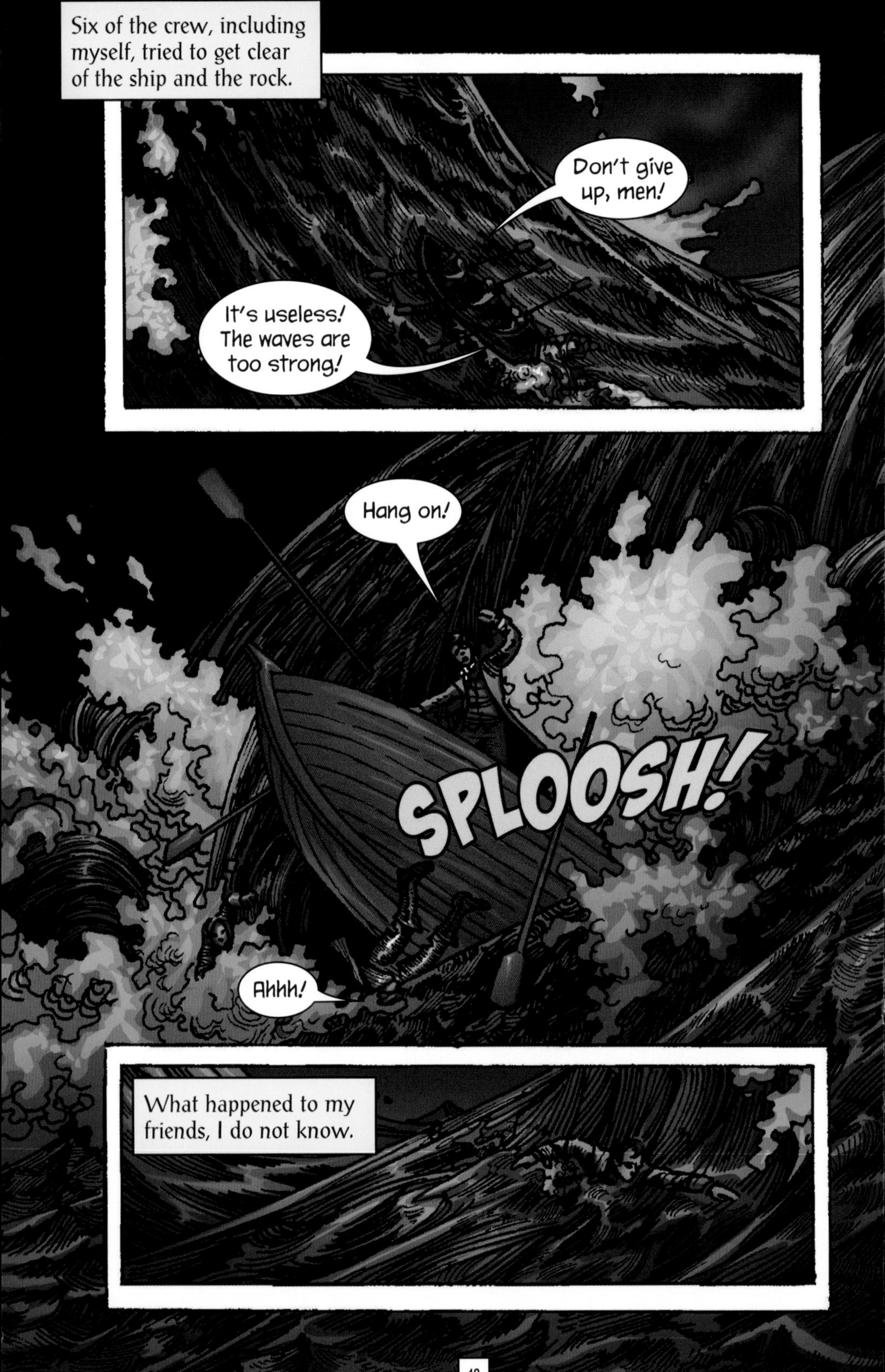
Six of the crew, including myself, tried to get clear of the ship and the rock.
Don't give up, men!
It's useless! The waves are too strong!
Hang on!
SPLOOSH!
Ahhh!
What happened to my friends, I do not know.

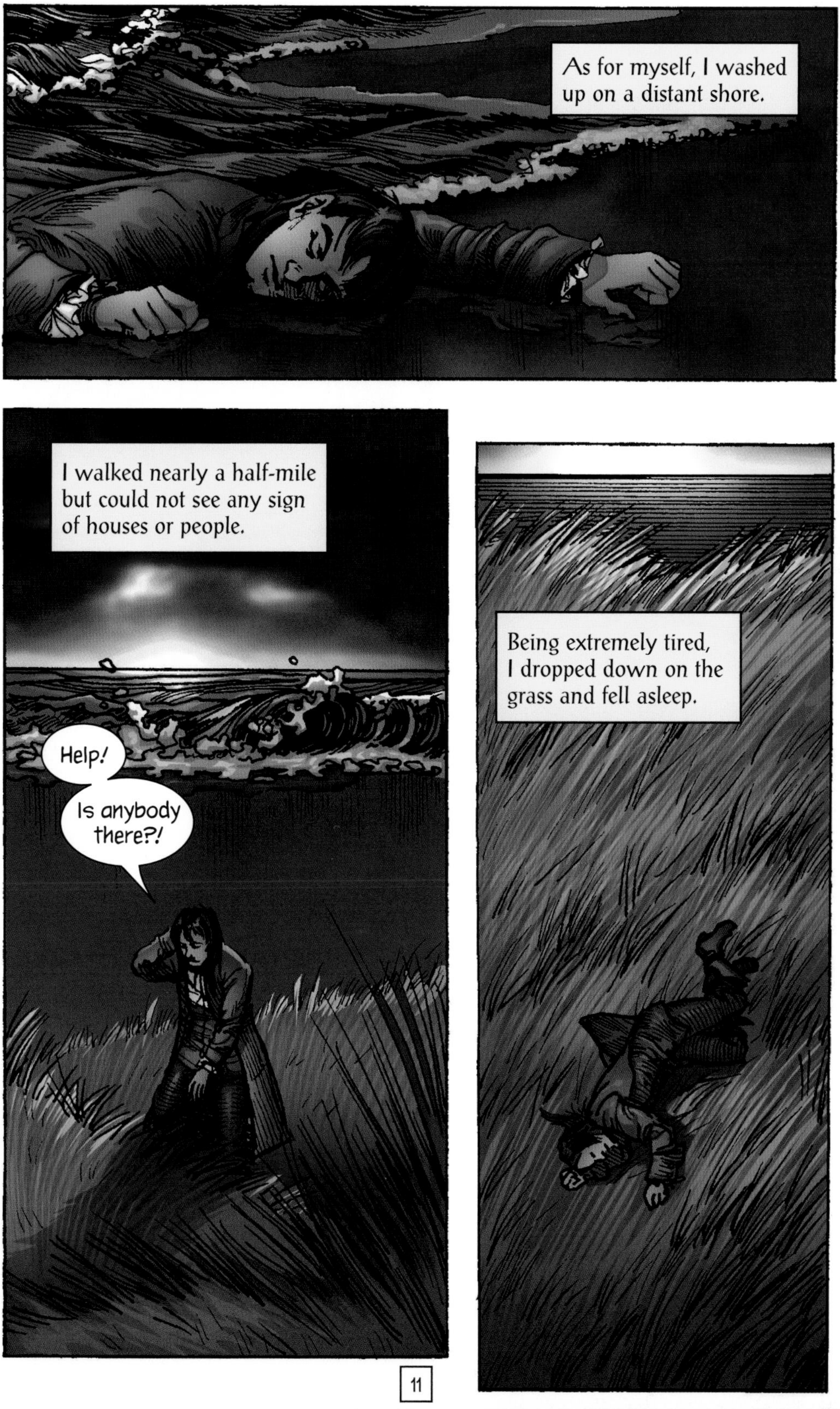
As for myself, I washed up on a distant shore.
I walked nearly a half-mile but could not see any sign of houses or people.
Help!
Is anybody there?!
Being extremely tired, I dropped down on the grass and fell asleep.

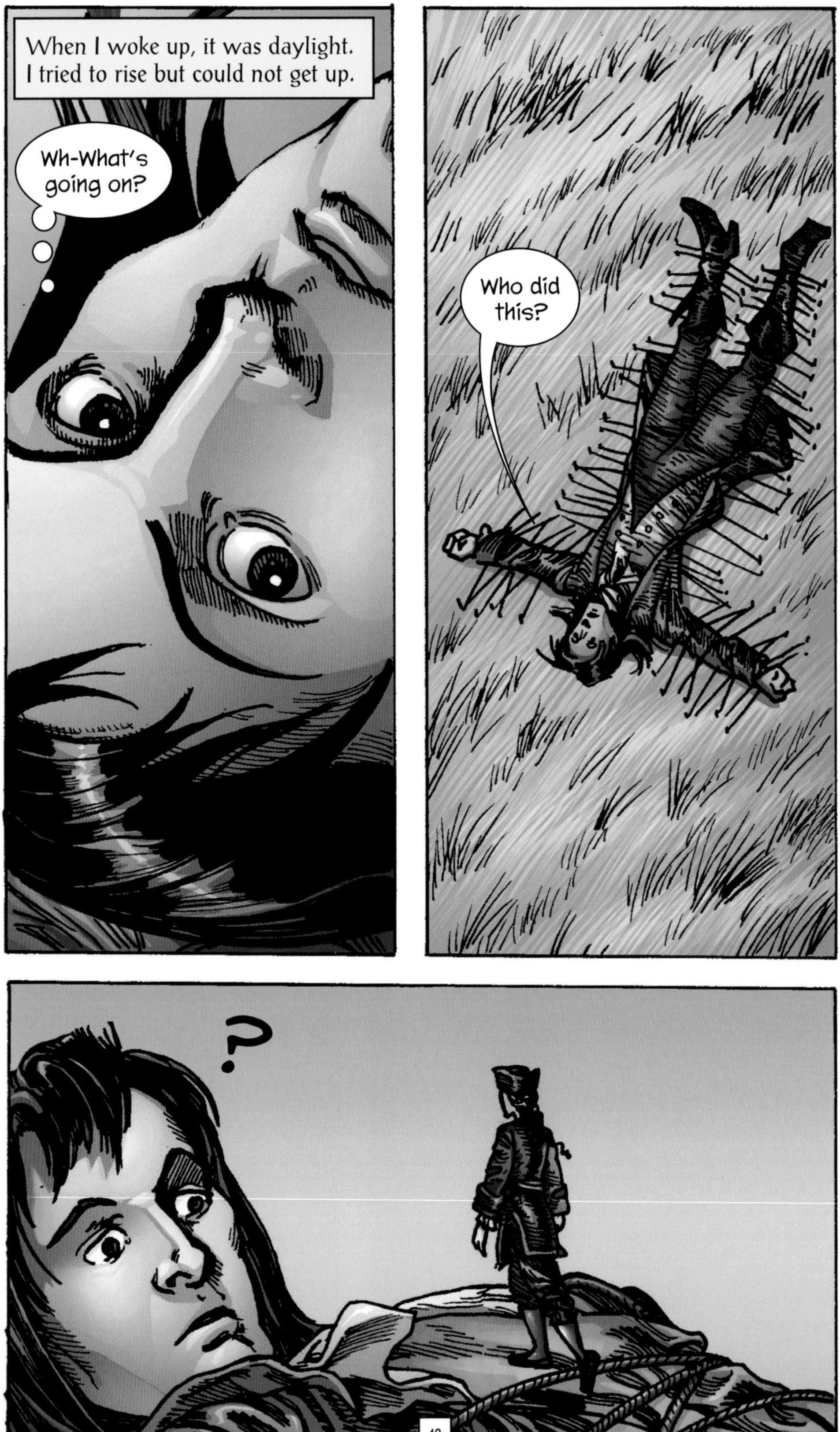
When I woke up, it was daylight. I tried to rise but could not get up.
Wh-What's going on?
Who did this?
?

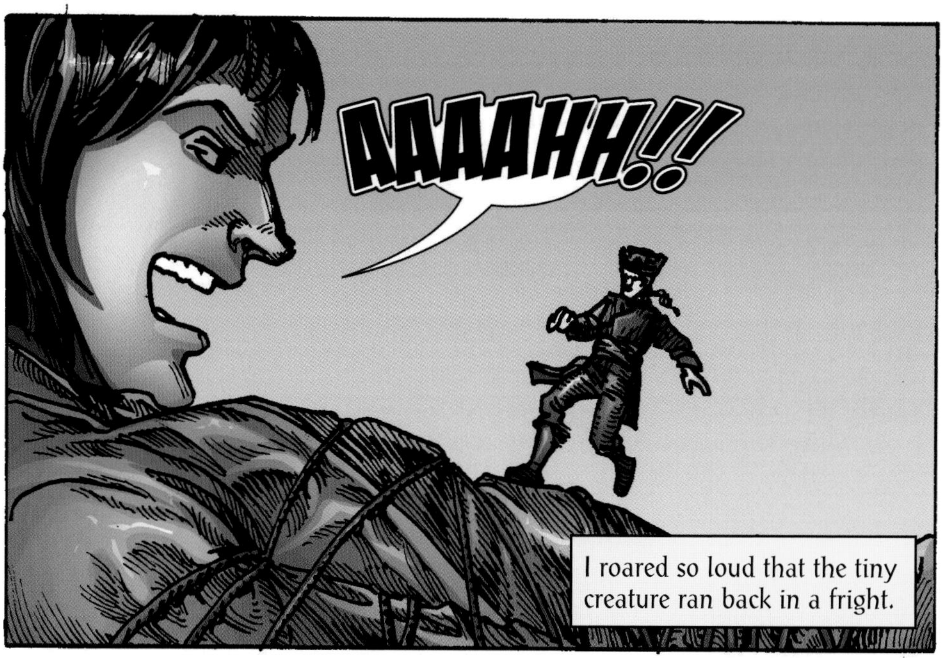
AAAAHH!!
I roared so loud that the tiny creature ran back in a fright.

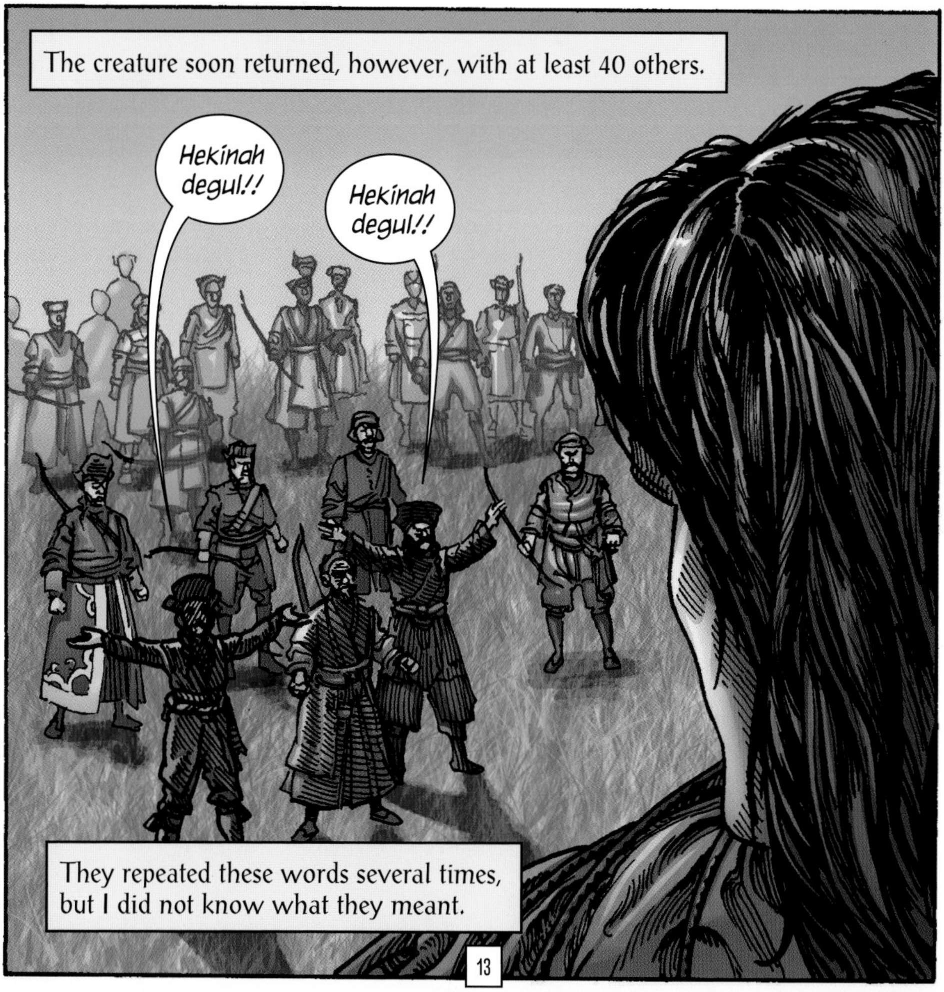
The creature soon returned, however, with at least 40 others.
Hekinah degul!!
Hekinah degul!!
They repeated these words several times, but I did not know what they meant.

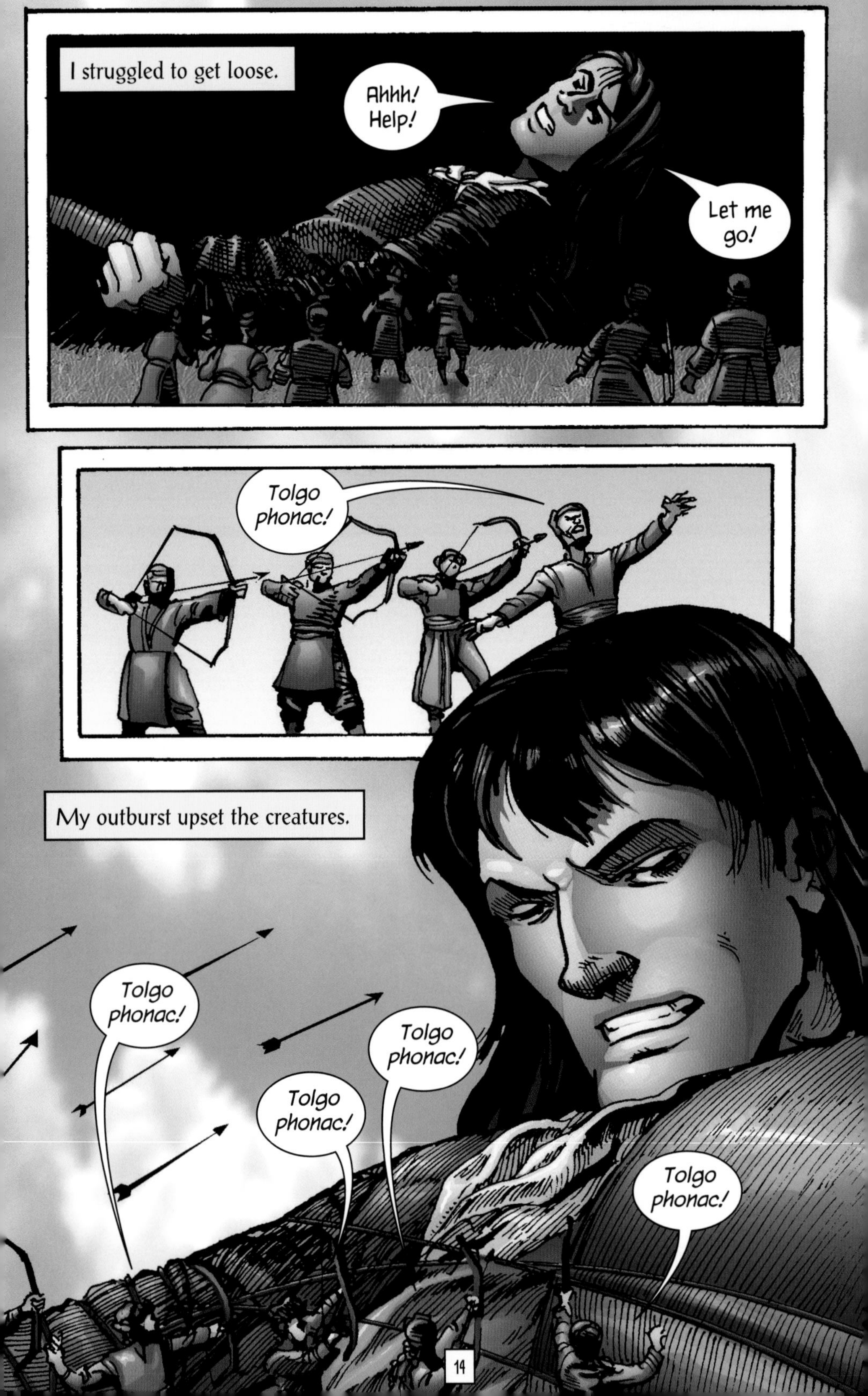

I struggled to get loose.
Ahhh! Help!
Let me go!
Tolgo phonac!
My outburst upset the creatures.
Tolgo phonac!
Tolgo phonac!
Tolgo phonac!
Tolgo phonac!

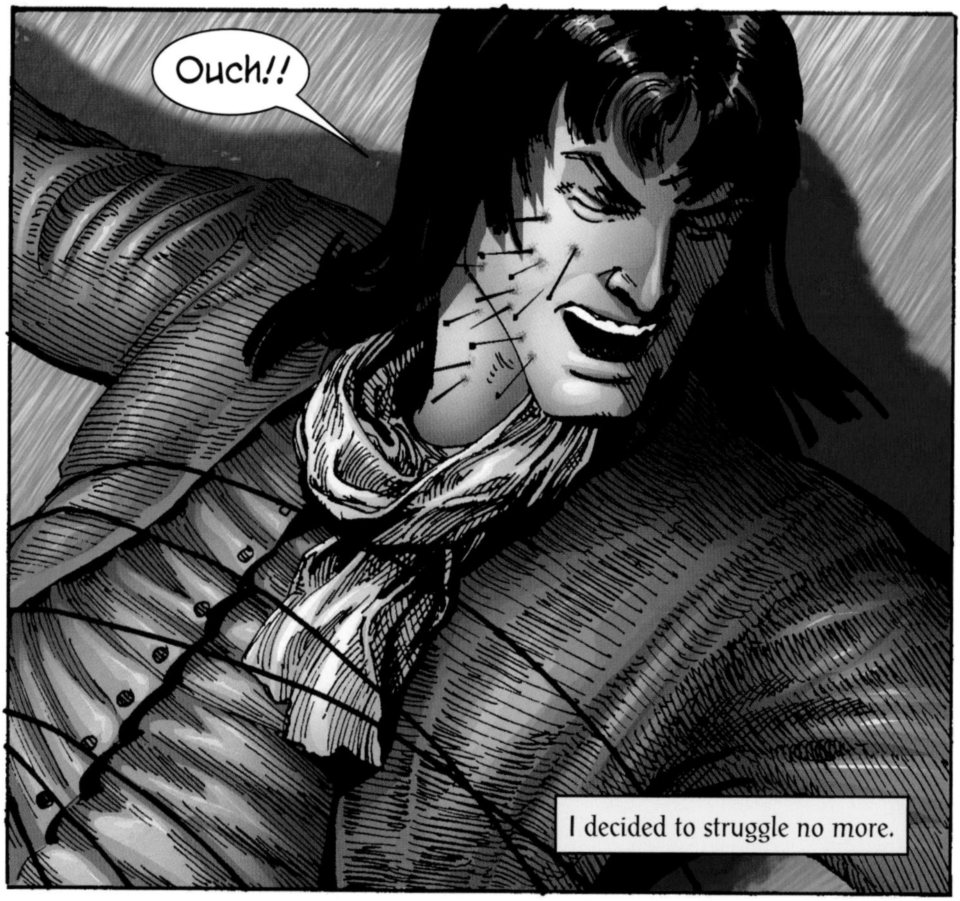
Ouch!!
I decided to struggle no more.

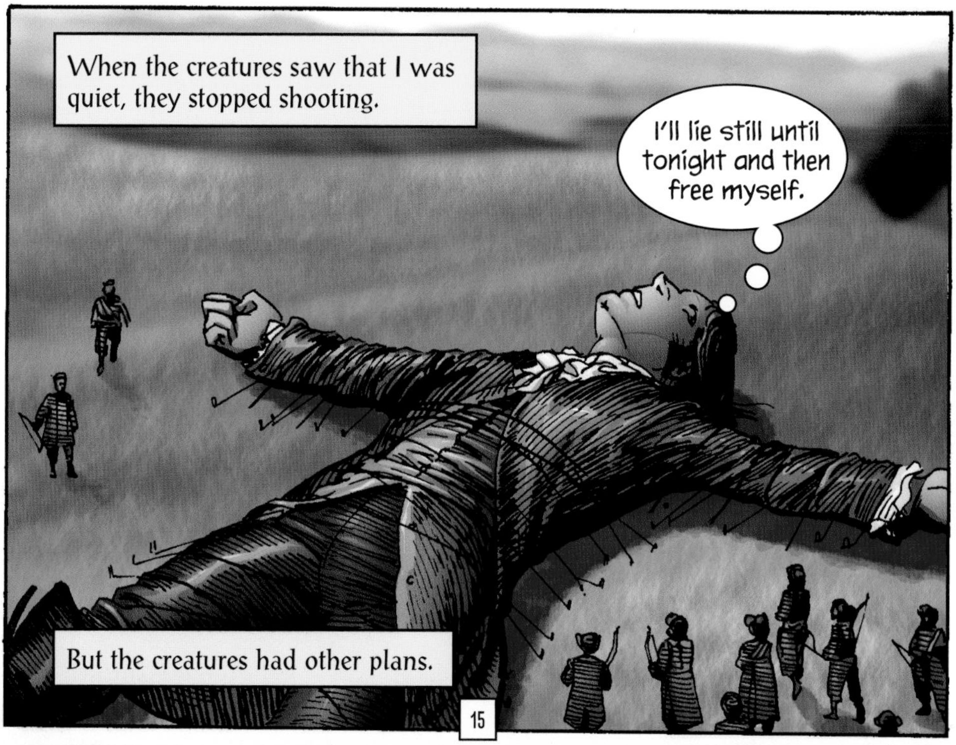
When the creatures saw that I was quiet, they stopped shooting.
I'll lie still until tonight and then free myself.
But the creatures had other plans.

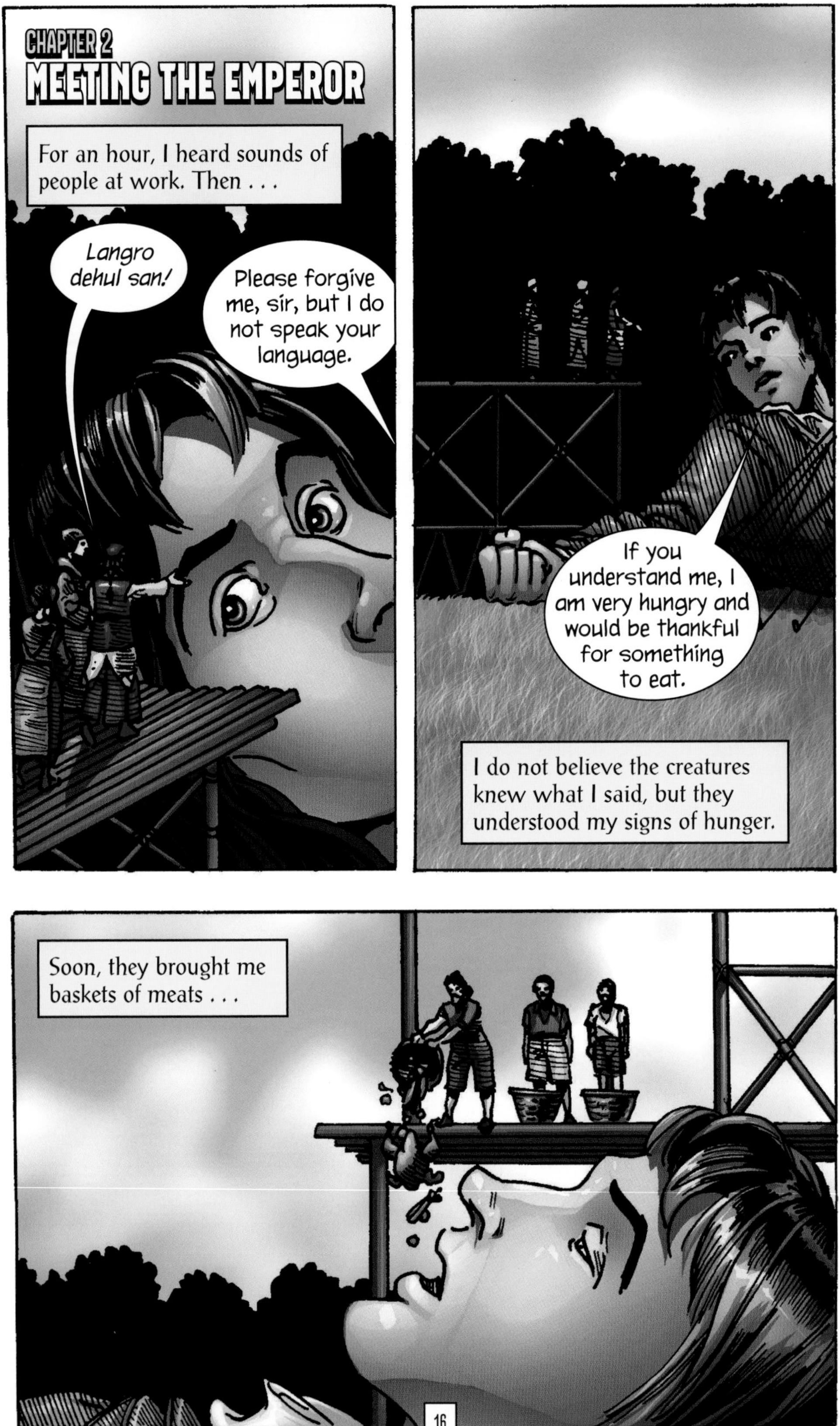

CHAPTER 2
MEETING THE EMPEROR
For an hour, I heard sounds of people at work. Then . . .
Langro dehul san!
Please forgive me, sir, but I do not speak your language.
If you understand me, I am very hungry and would be thankful for something to eat.
I do not believe the creatures knew what I said, but they understood my signs of hunger.
Soon, they brought me baskets of meats . . .

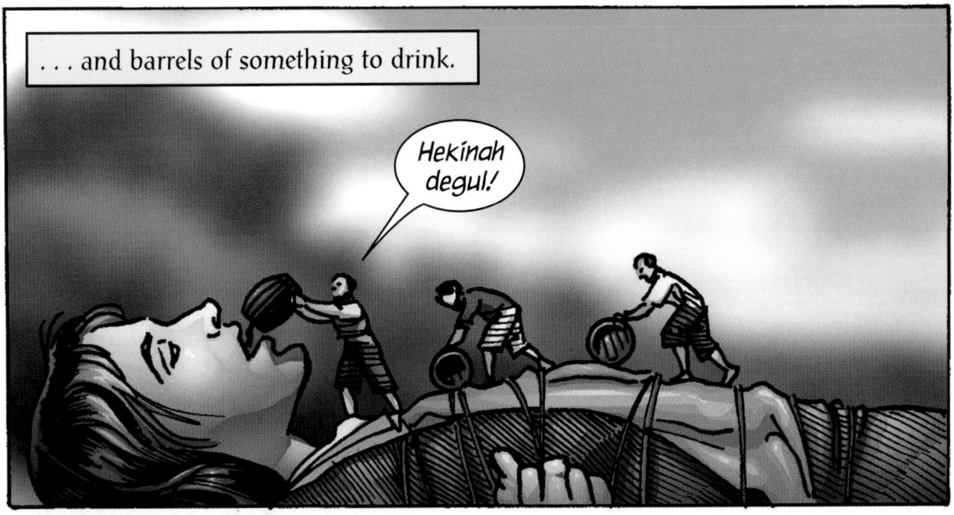
. . . and barrels of something to drink.
Hekinah degul!

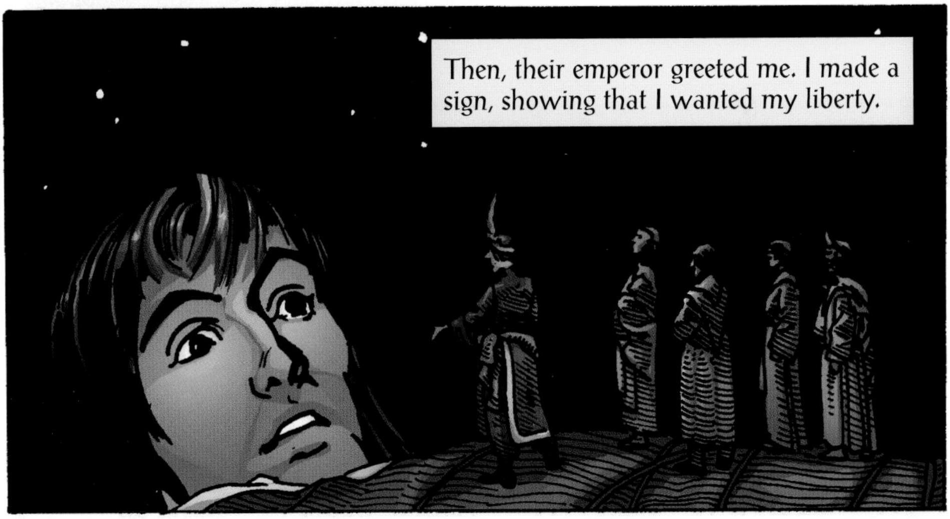
Then, their emperor greeted me. I made a sign, showing that I wanted my liberty.

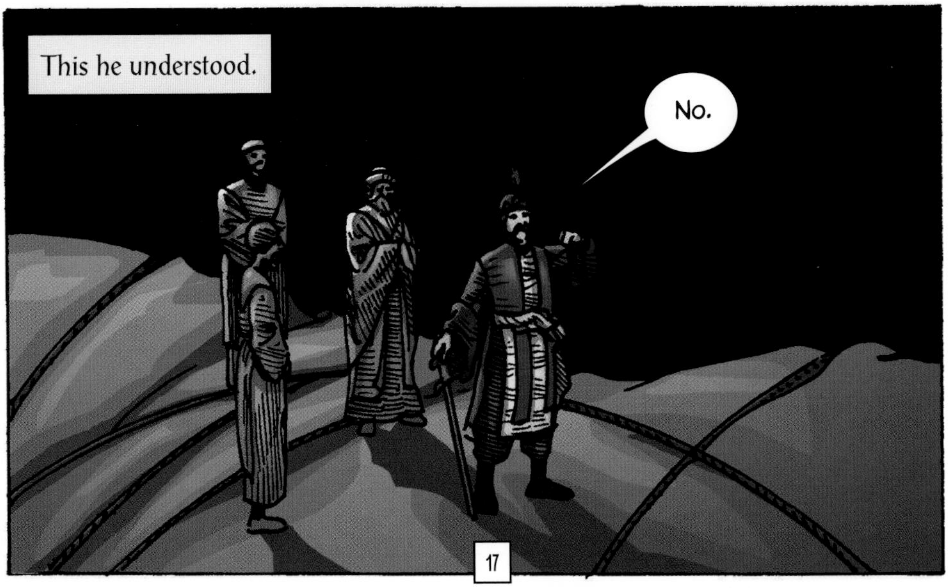
This he understood.
No.

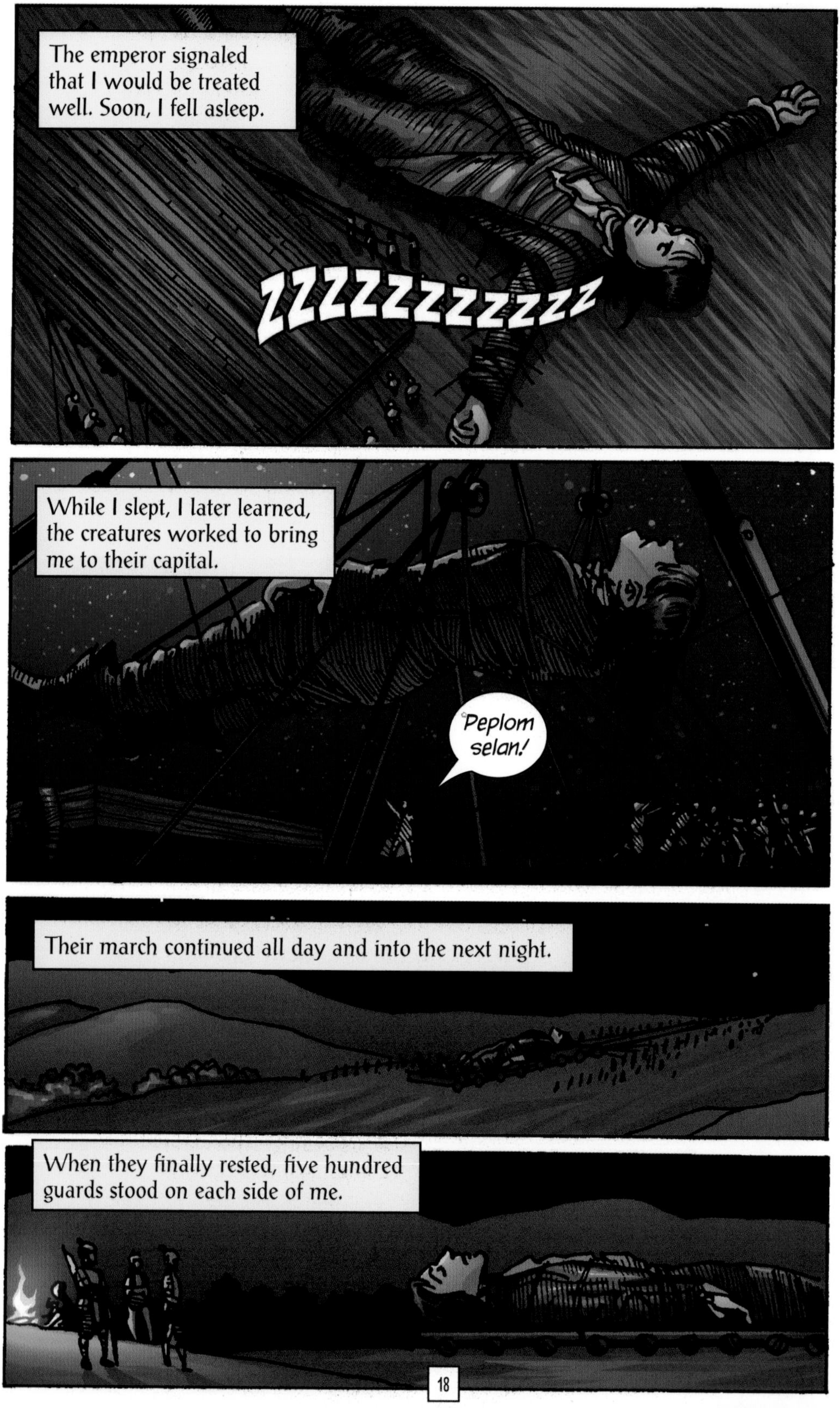

The emperor signaled that I would be treated well. Soon, I fell asleep.
ZZZZZZZZZZZZ
While I slept, I later learned, the creatures worked to bring me to their capital.
Peplom selan!
Their march continued all day and into the next night.
When they finally rested, five hundred guards stood on each side of me.

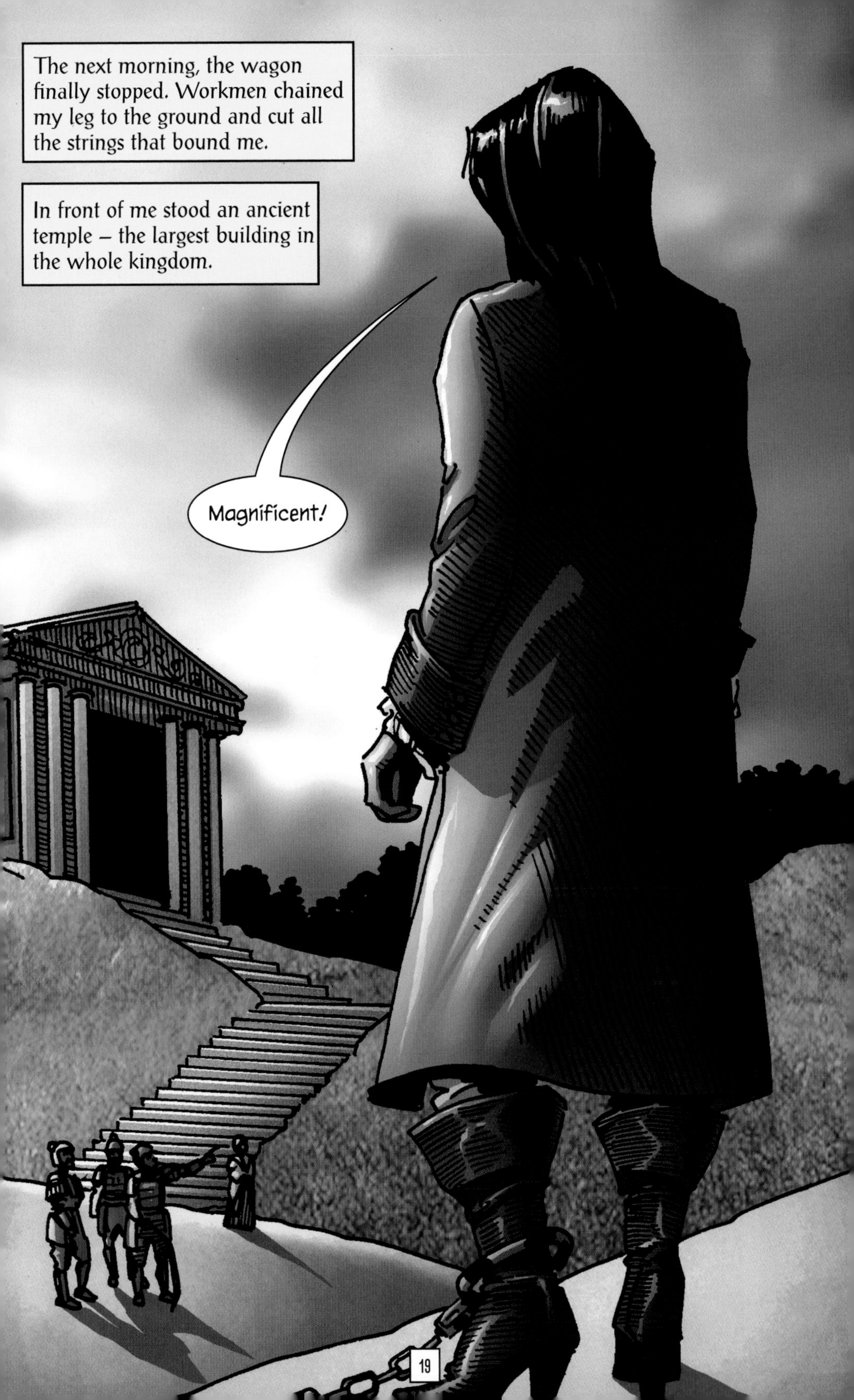
The next morning, the wagon finally stopped. Workmen chained my leg to the ground and cut all the strings that bound me.
In front of me stood an ancient temple – the largest building in the whole kingdom.
Magnificent!

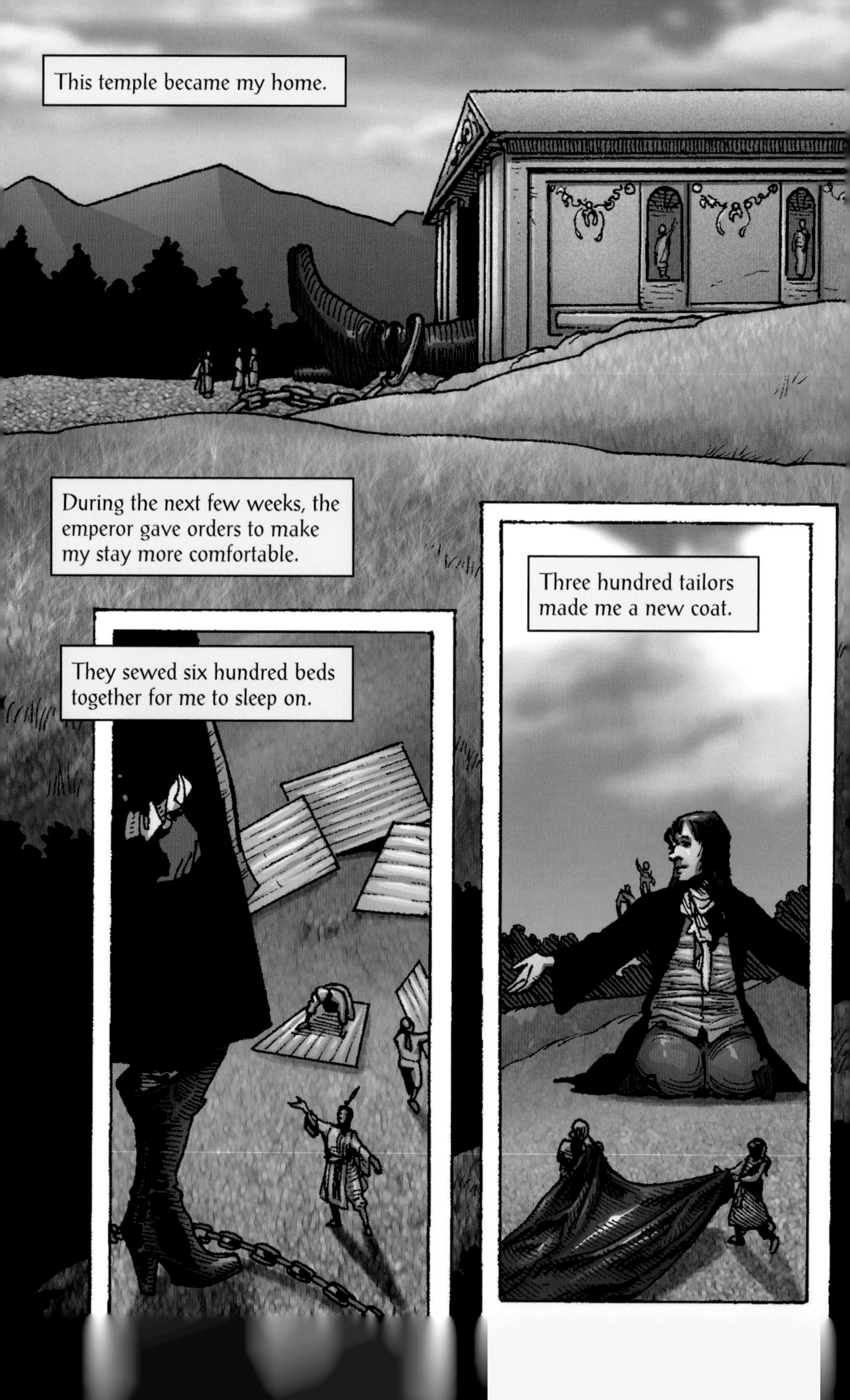
This temple became my home.
During the next few weeks, the emperor gave orders to make my stay more comfortable.
They sewed six hundred beds together for me to sleep on.
Three hundred tailors made me a new coat.

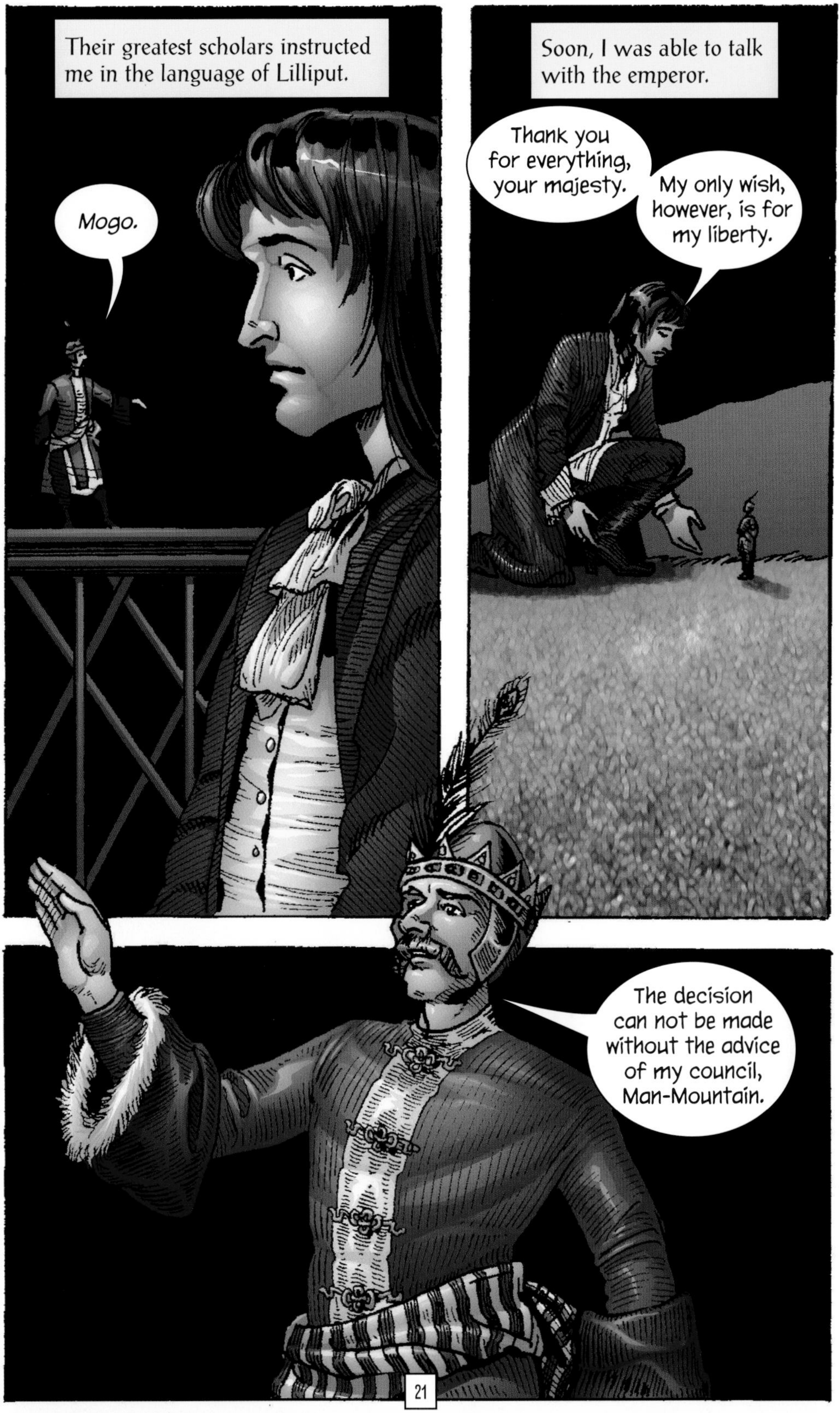
Their greatest scholars instructed me in the language of Lilliput.
Mogo.
Soon, I was able to talk with the emperor.
Thank you for everything, your majesty.
My only wish, however, is for my liberty.
The decision can not be made without the advice of my council, Man-Mountain.

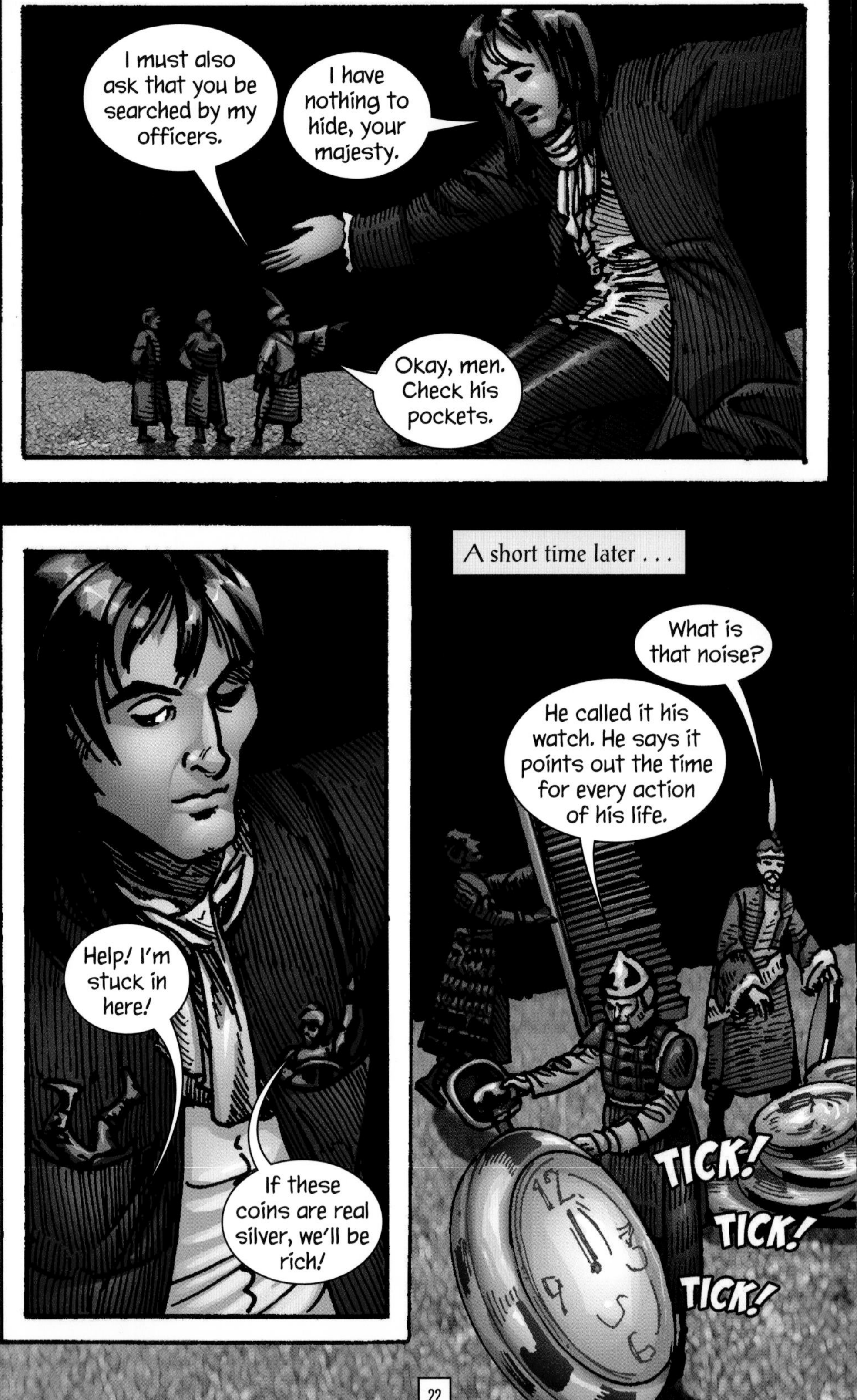
I must also ask that you be searched by my officers.
I have nothing to hide, your majesty.
Okay, men. Check his pockets.
A short time later . . .
Help! I'm stuck in here!
If these coins are real silver, we'll be rich!
What is that noise?
He called it his watch. He says it points out the time for every action of his life.
TICK!
TICK!
TICK!

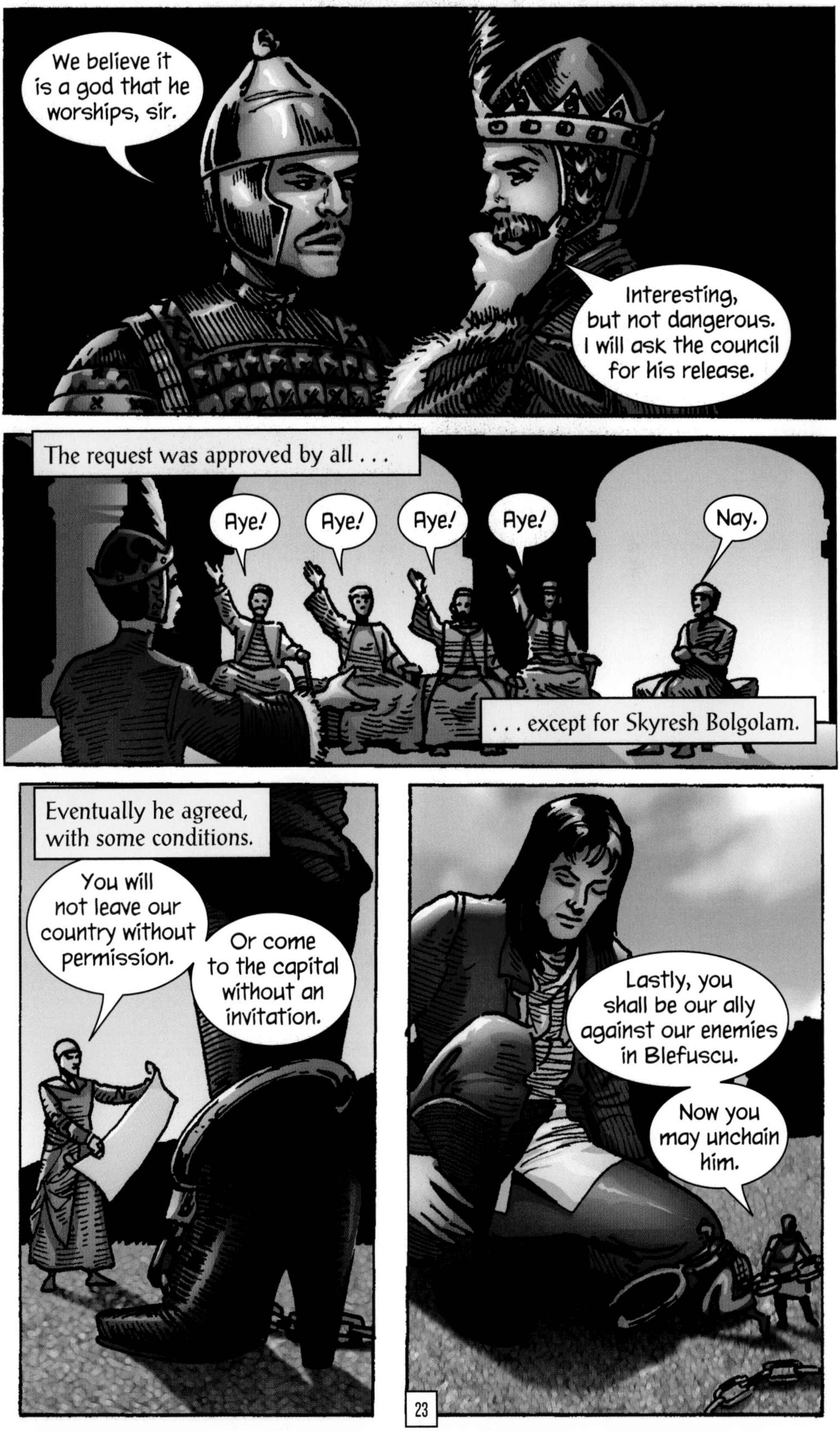
We believe it is a god that he worships, sir.
Interesting, but not dangerous. I will ask the council for his release.
The request was approved by all . . .
Aye!
Aye!
Aye!
Aye!
Nay.
. . . except for Skyresh Bolgolam.
Eventually he agreed, with some conditions.
You will not leave our country without permission.
Or come to the capital without an invitation.
Lastly, you shall be our ally against our enemies in Blefuscu.
Now you may unchain him.

CHAPTER 3
THE WAR WITH BLEFUSCU

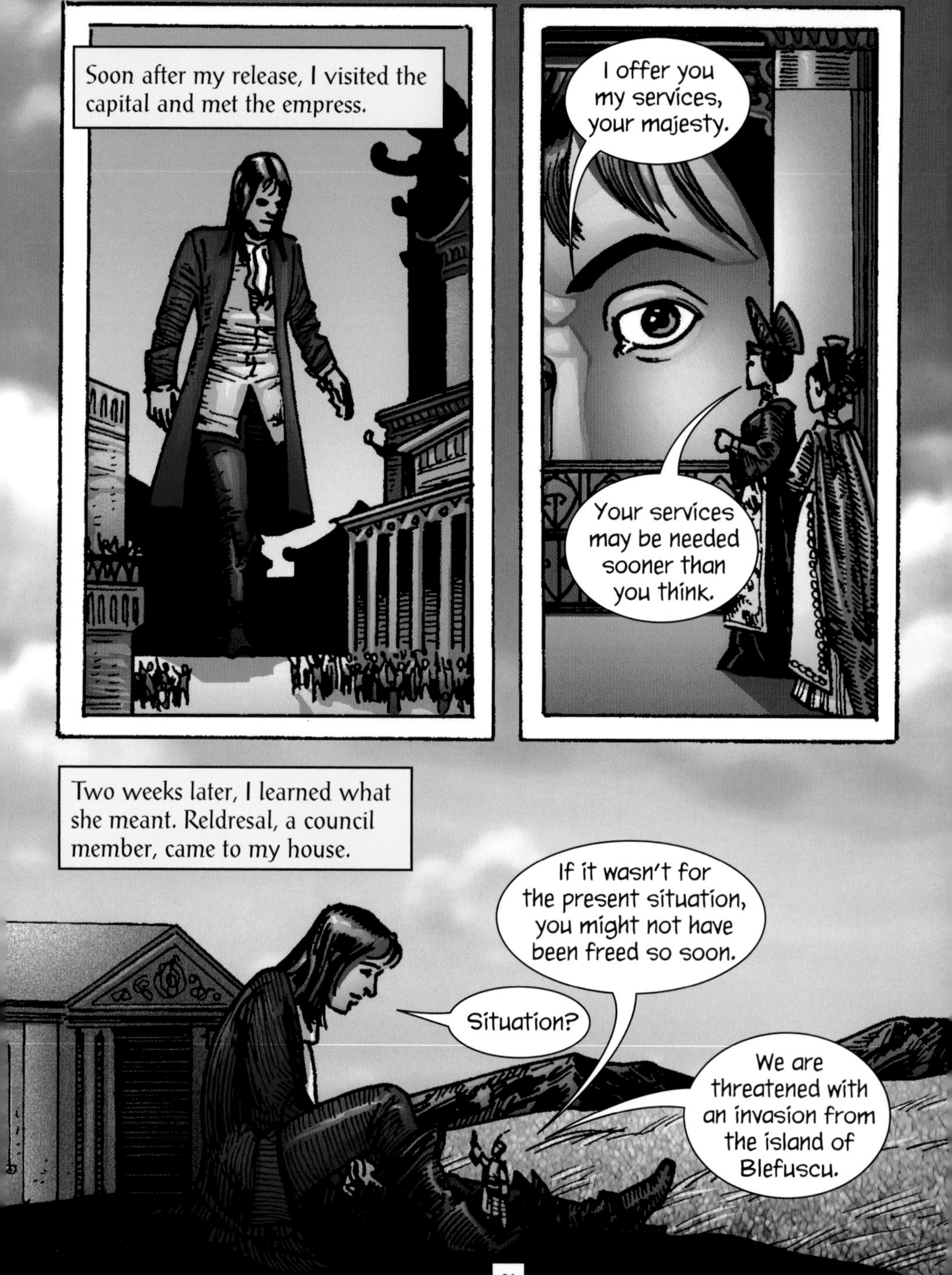
Soon after my release, I visited the capital and met the empress.
I offer you my services, your majesty.
Your services may be needed sooner than you think.
Two weeks later, I learned what she meant. Reldresal, a council member, came to my house.
If it wasn't for the present situation, you might not have been freed so soon.
Situation?
We are threatened with an invasion from the island of Blefuscu.

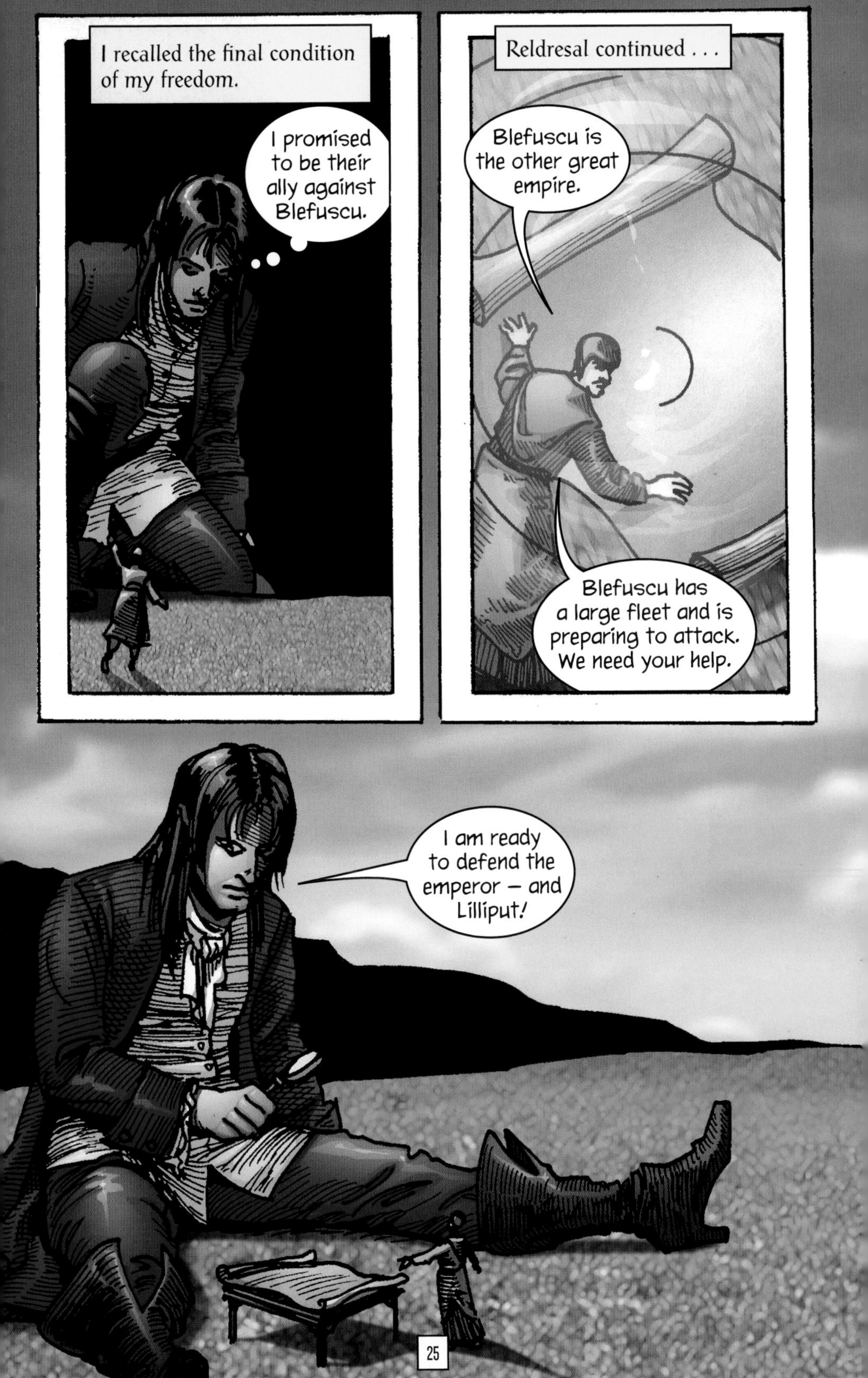
I recalled the final condition of my freedom.
I promised to be their ally against Blefuscu.
Reldresal continued . . .
Blefuscu is the other great empire.
Blefuscu has a large fleet and is preparing to attack. We need your help.
I am ready to defend the emperor – and Lilliput!

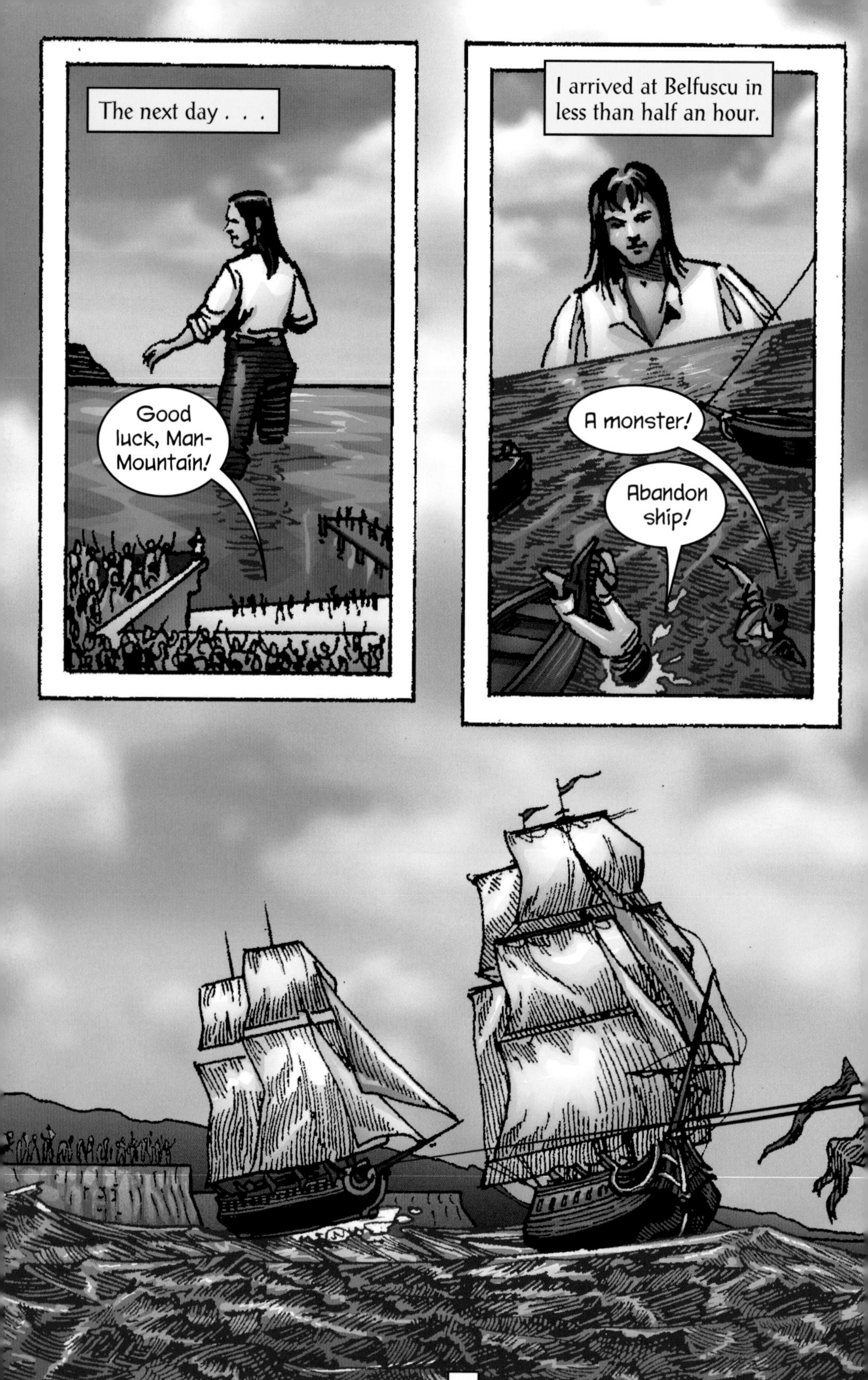
The next day . . .
Good luck, Man-Mountain!
I arrived at Belfuscu in less than half an hour.
A monster!
Abandon ship!

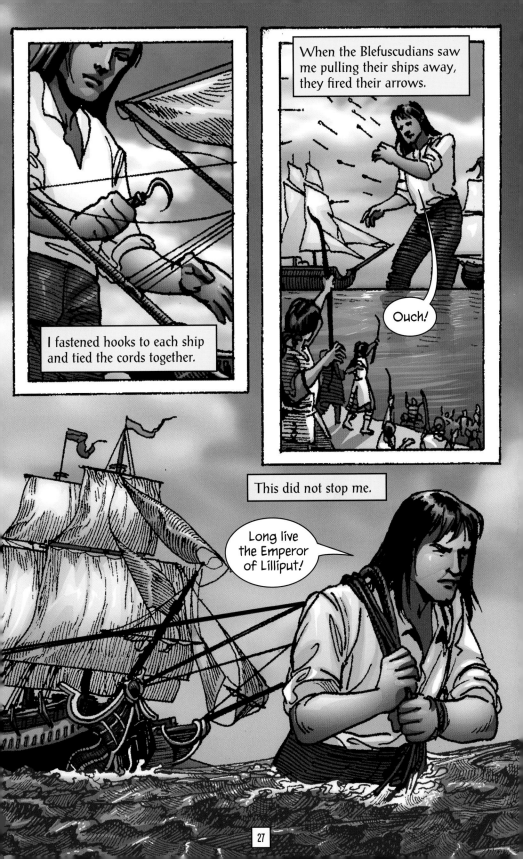

I fastened hooks to each ship and tied the cords together.

When the Blefuscudians saw me pulling their ships away, they fired their arrows.

Ouch!

This did not stop me.

Long live the Emperor of Lilliput!

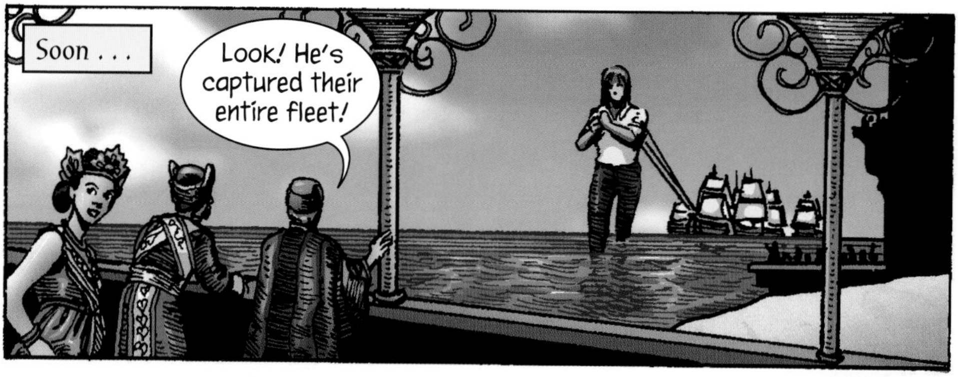
Soon . . .
Look! He's captured their entire fleet!

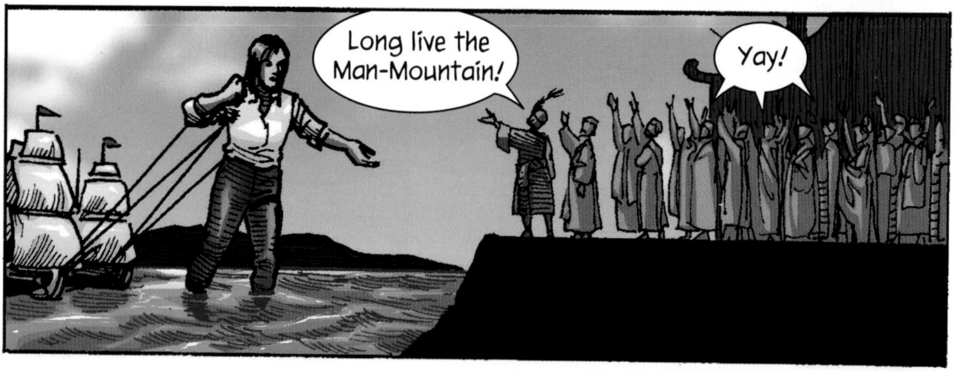
Long live the Man-Mountain!
Yay!

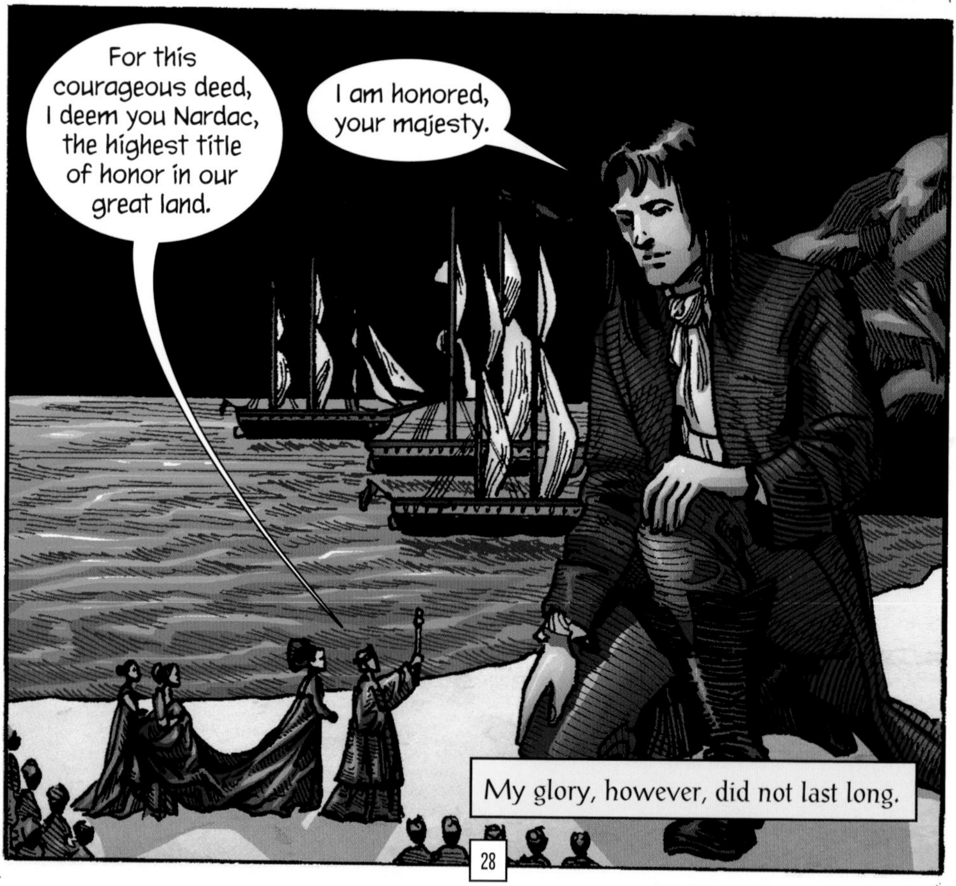
For this courageous deed, I deem you Nardac, the highest title of honor in our great land.
I am honored, your majesty.
My glory, however, did not last long.

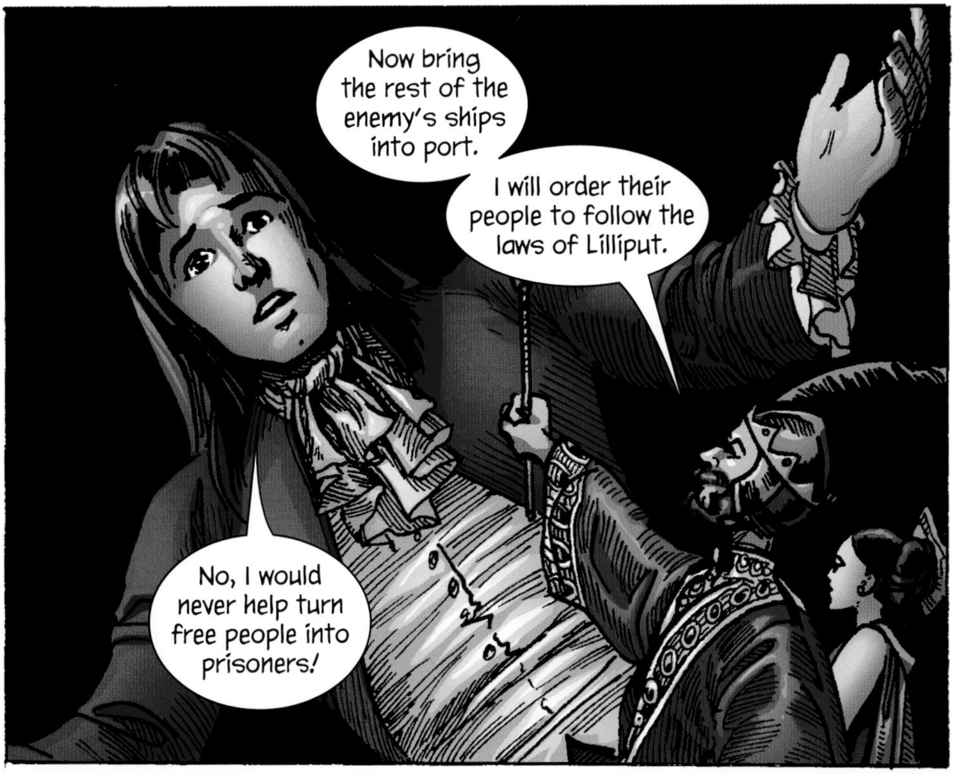
Now bring the rest of the enemy's ships into port.
I will order their people to follow the laws of Lilliput.
No, I would never help turn free people into prisoners!

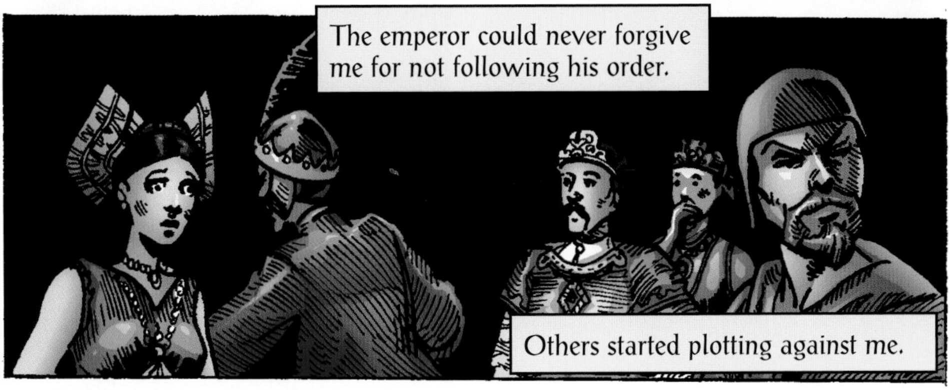
The emperor could never forgive me for not following his order.
Others started plotting against me.

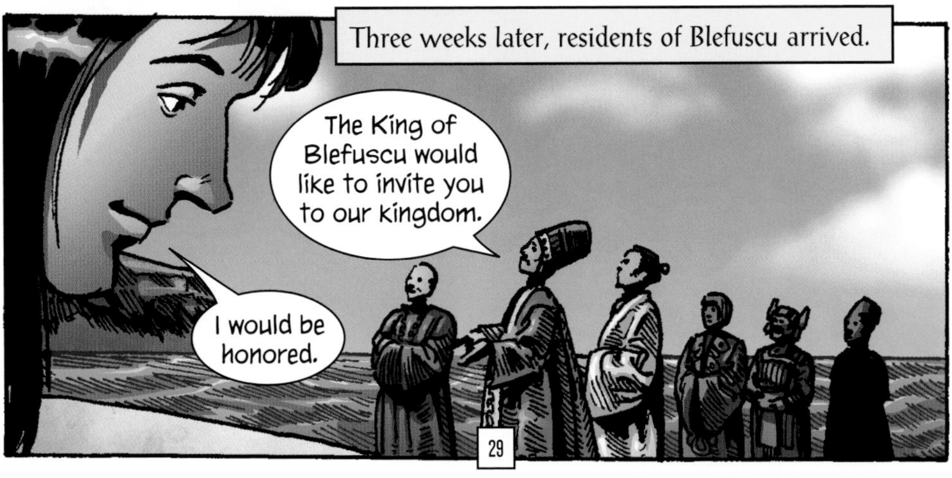
Three weeks later, residents of Blefuscu arrived.
The King of Blefuscu would like to invite you to our kingdom.
I would be honored.

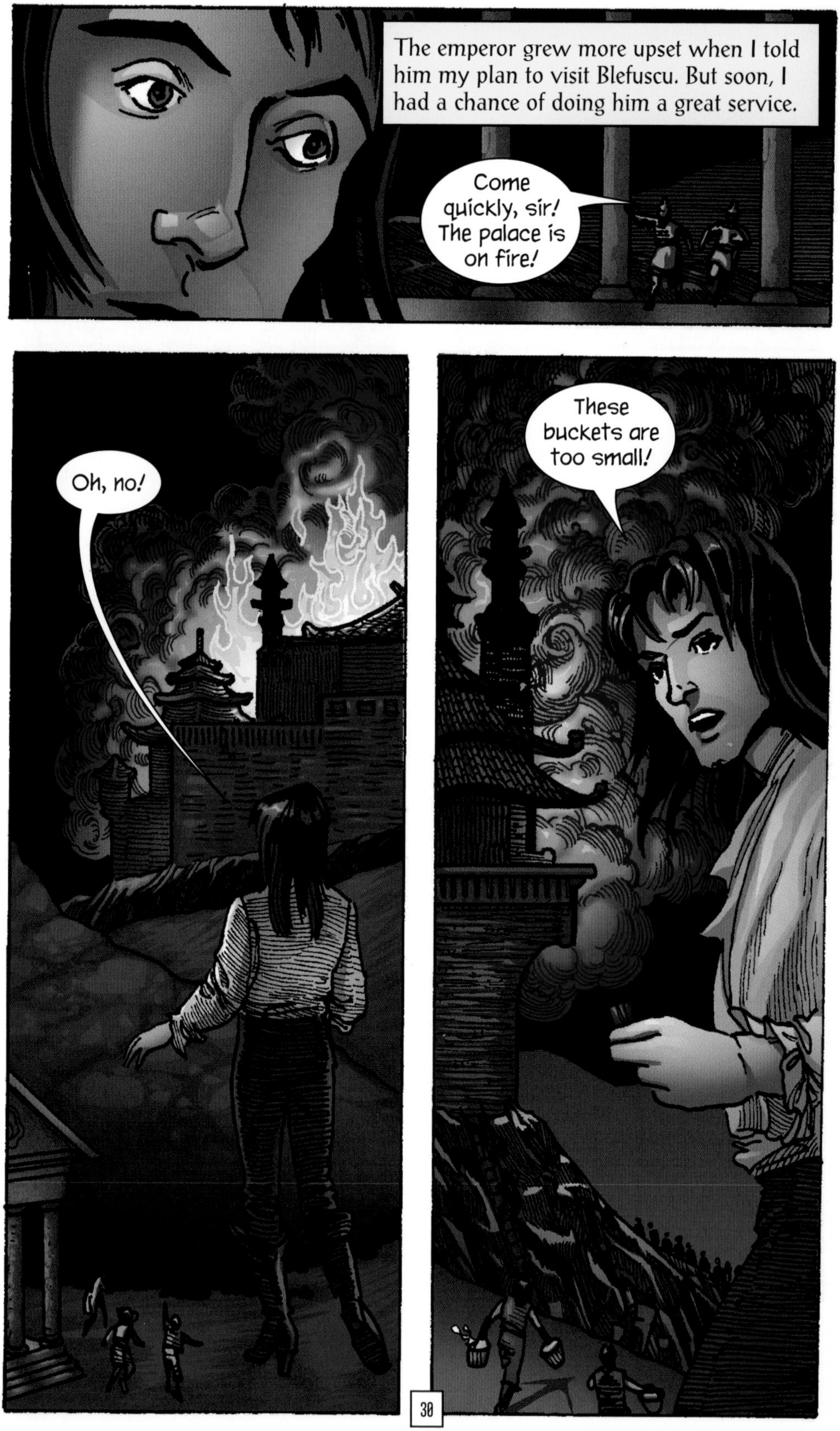
The emperor grew more upset when I told him my plan to visit Blefuscu. But soon, I had a chance of doing him a great service.
Come quickly, sir! The palace is on fire!
Oh, no!
These buckets are too small!

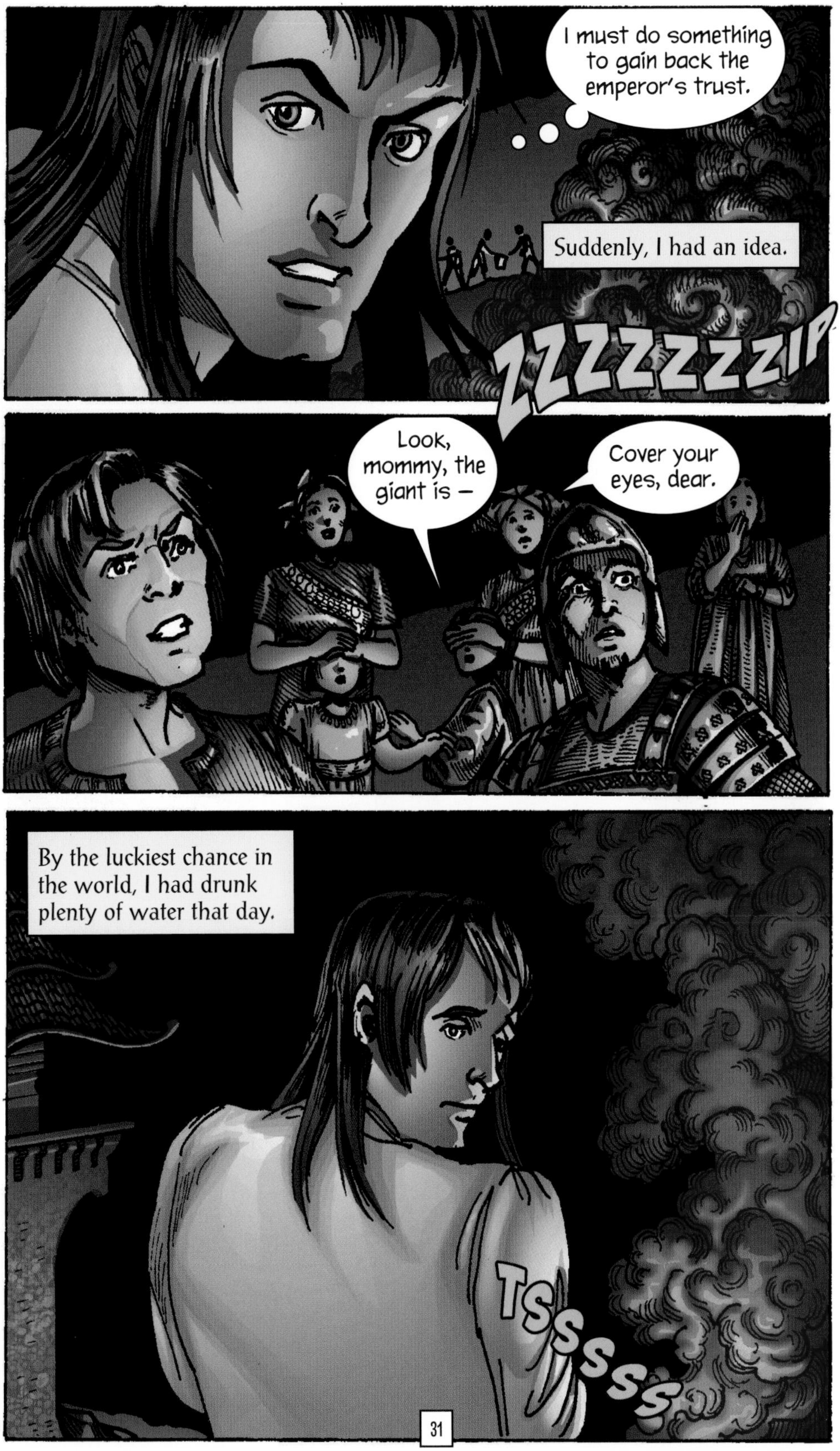
I must do something to gain back the emperor's trust.
Suddenly, I had an idea.
ZZZZZZZZIP
Look, mommy, the giant is –
Cover your eyes, dear.
By the luckiest chance in the world, I had drunk plenty of water that day.
TSSSSSS

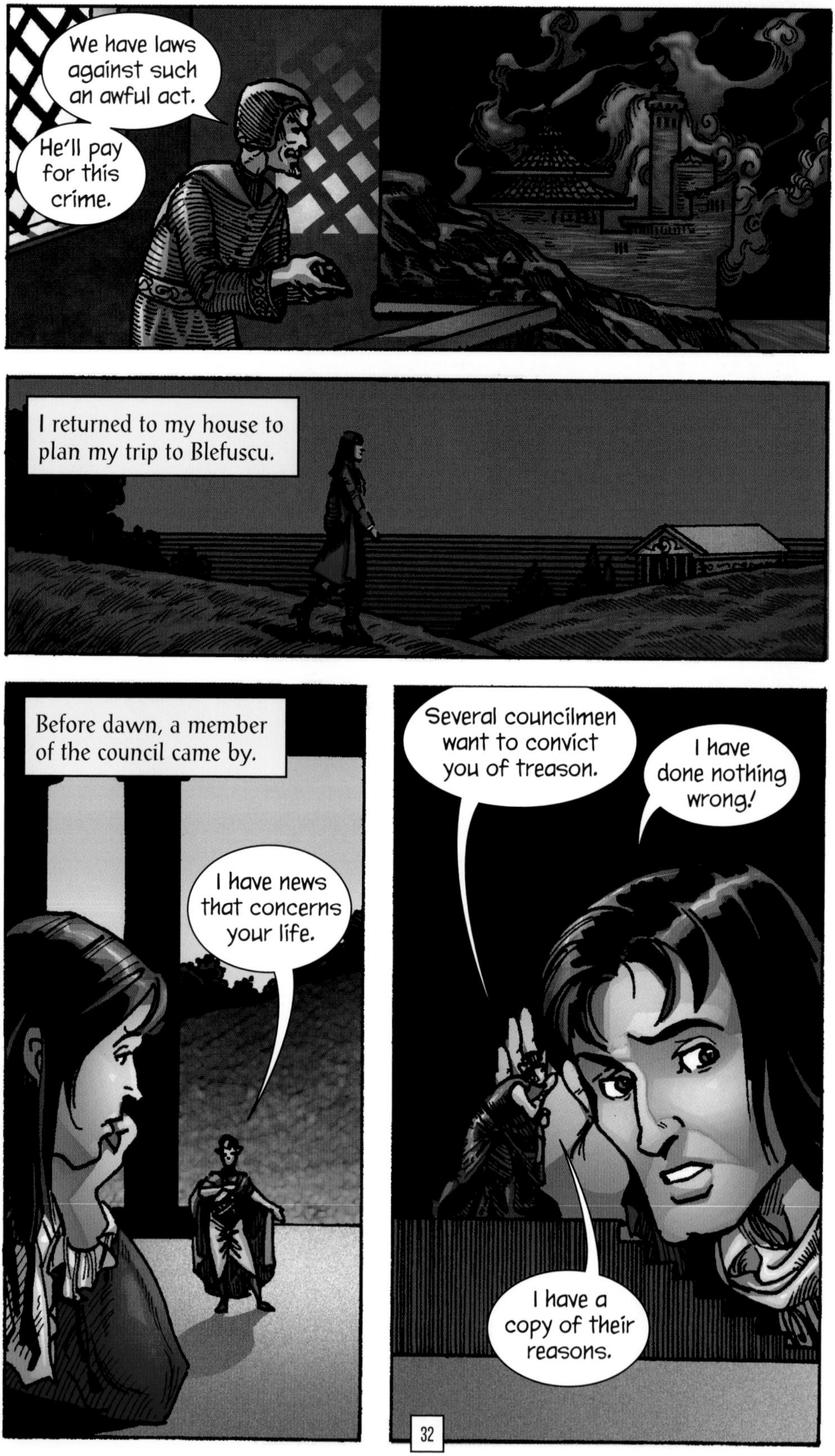
We have laws against such an awful act.
He'll pay for this crime.
I returned to my house to plan my trip to Blefuscu.
Before dawn, a member of the council came by.
I have news that concerns your life.
Several councilmen want to convict you of treason.
I have done nothing wrong!
I have a copy of their reasons.

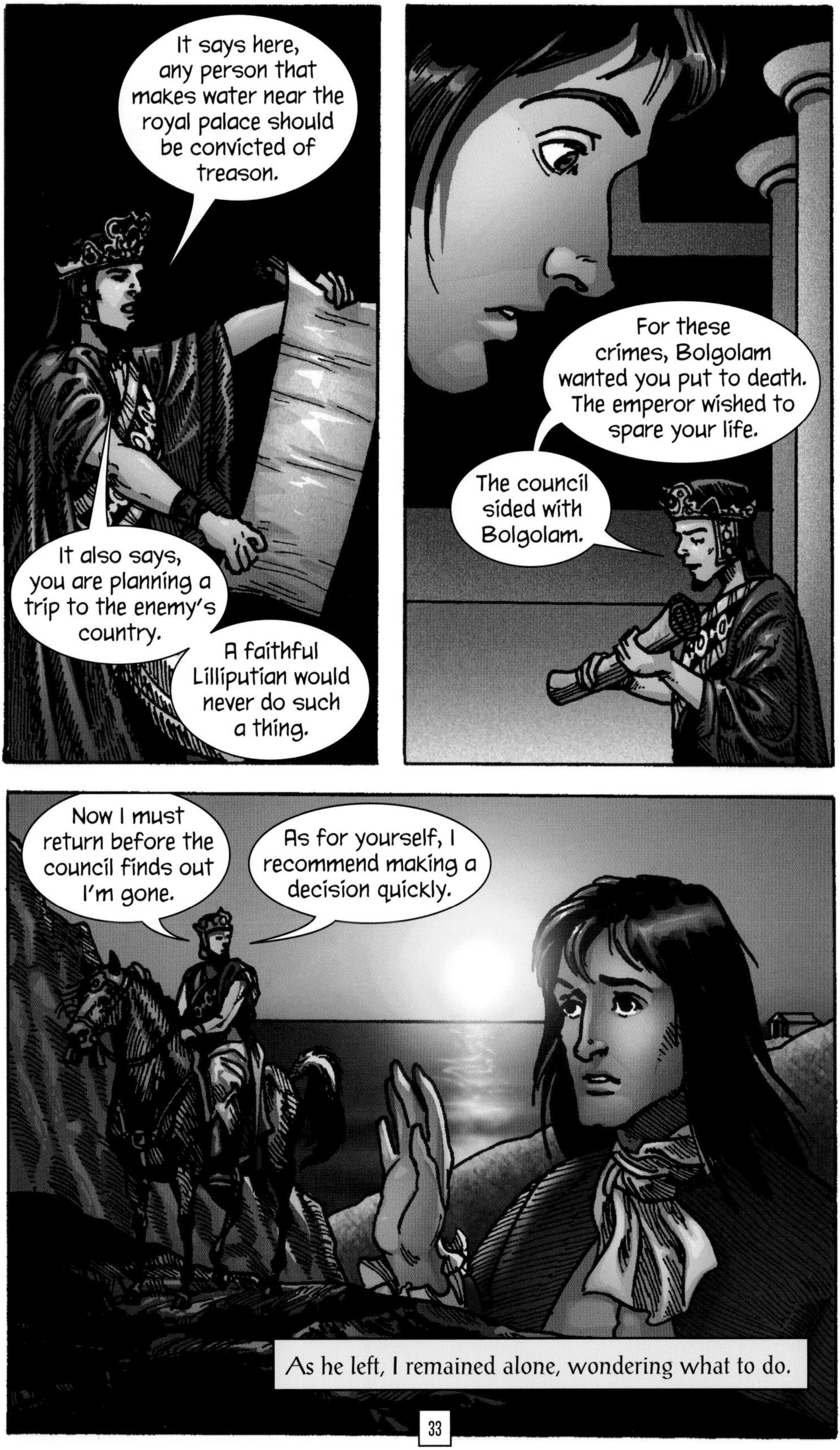
It says here, any person that makes water near the royal palace should be convicted of treason.
It also says, you are planning a trip to the enemy's country.
A faithful Lilliputian would never do such a thing.
For these crimes, Bolgolam wanted you put to death. The emperor wished to spare your life.
The council sided with Bolgolam.
Now I must return before the council finds out I'm gone.
As for yourself, I recommend making a decision quickly.
As he left, I remained alone, wondering what to do.

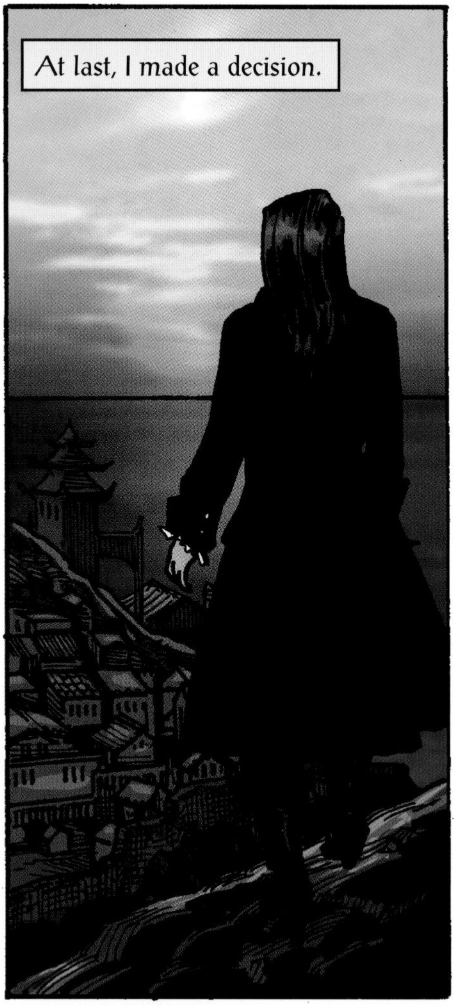
At last, I made a decision.

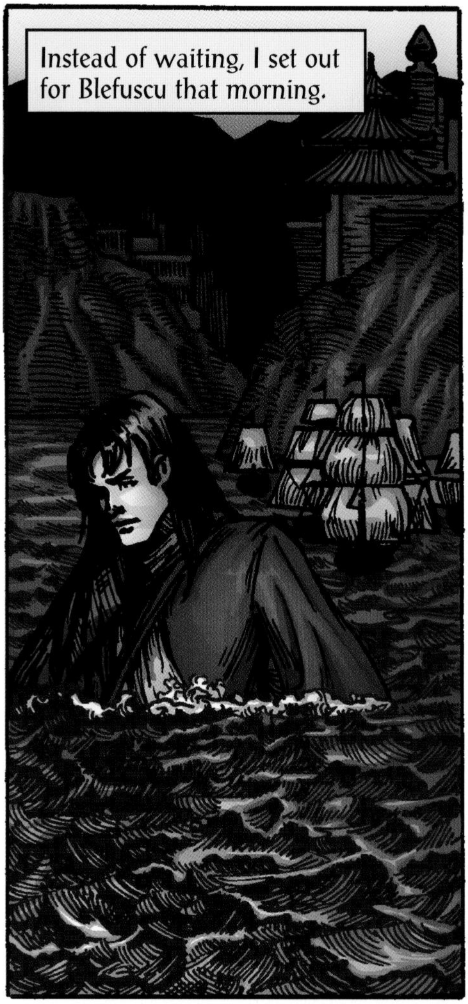
Instead of waiting, I set out for Blefuscu that morning.

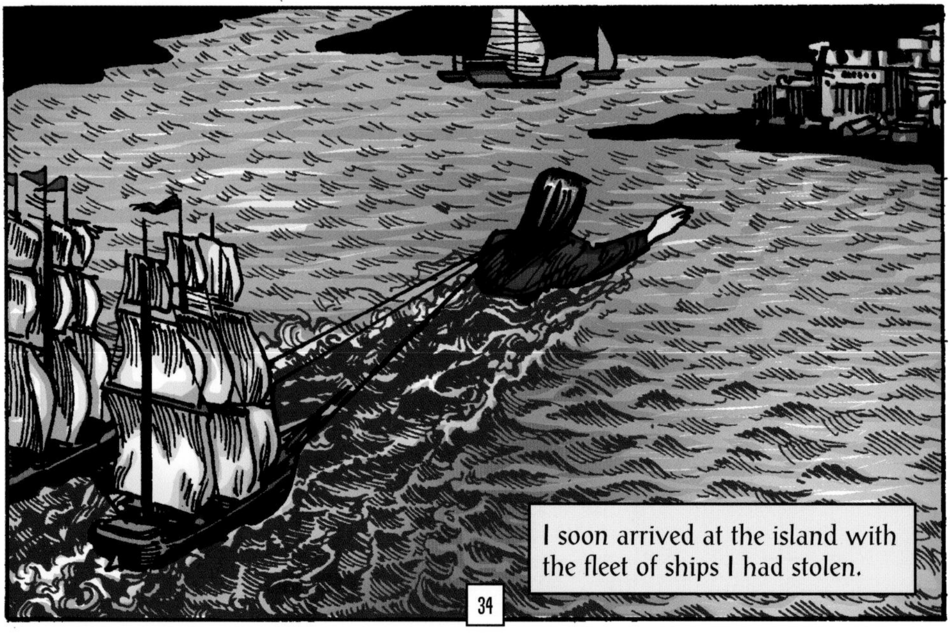
I soon arrived at the island with the fleet of ships I had stolen.

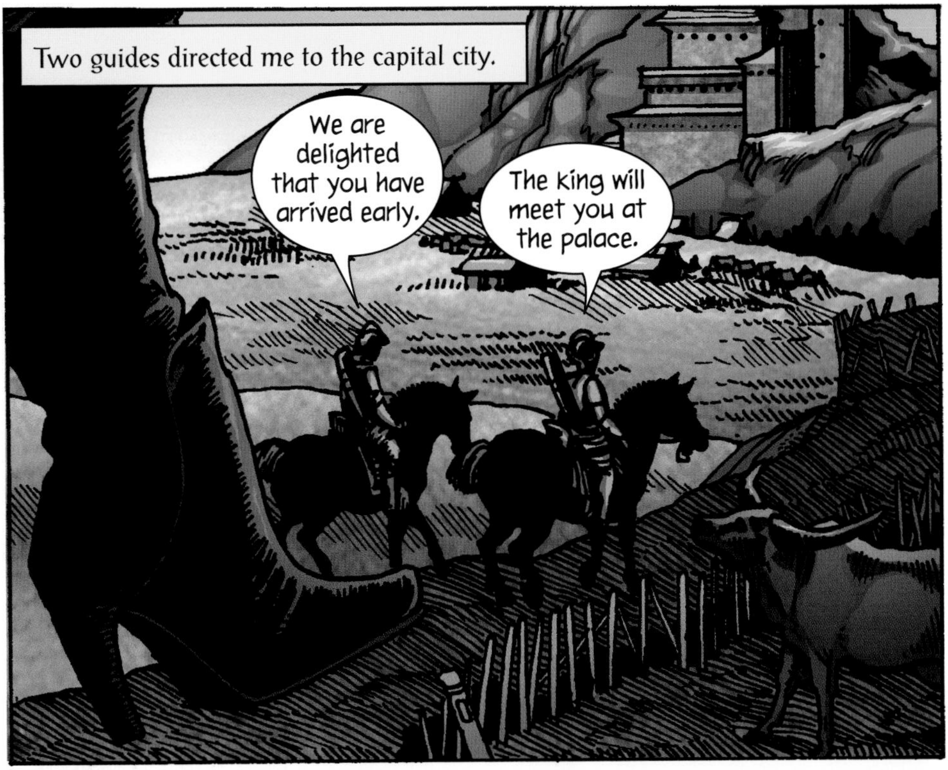
Two guides directed me to the capital city.
We are delighted that you have arrived early.
The king will meet you at the palace.

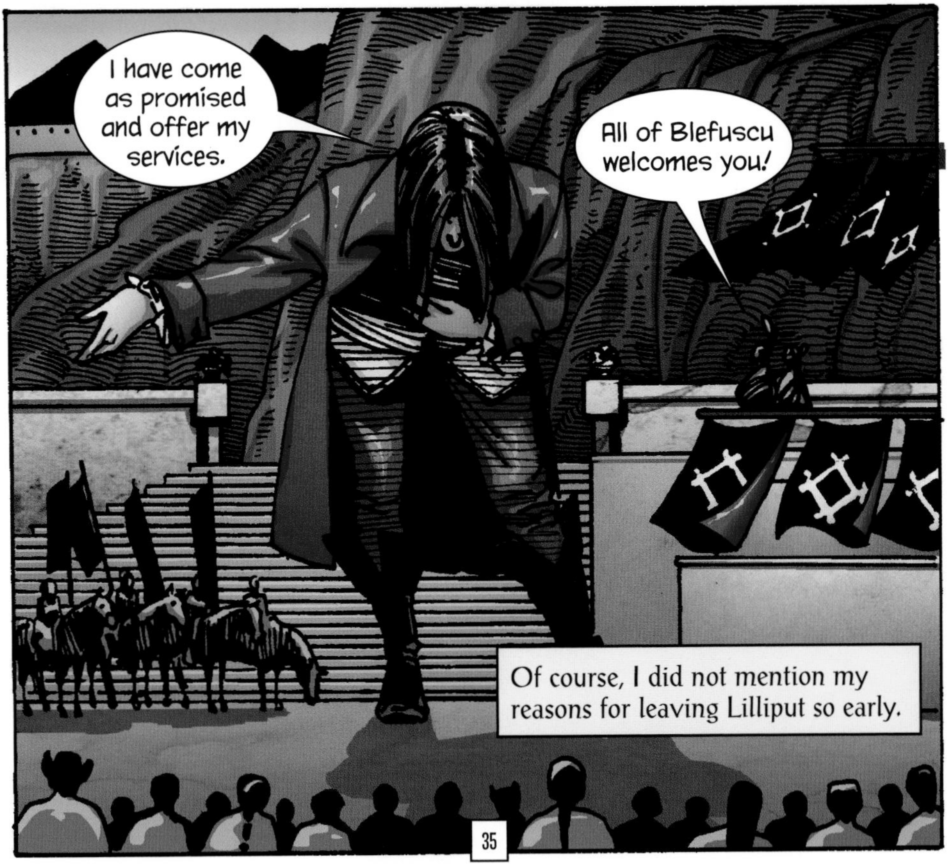
I have come as promised and offer my services.
All of Blefuscu welcomes you!
Of course, I did not mention my reasons for leaving Lilliput so early.

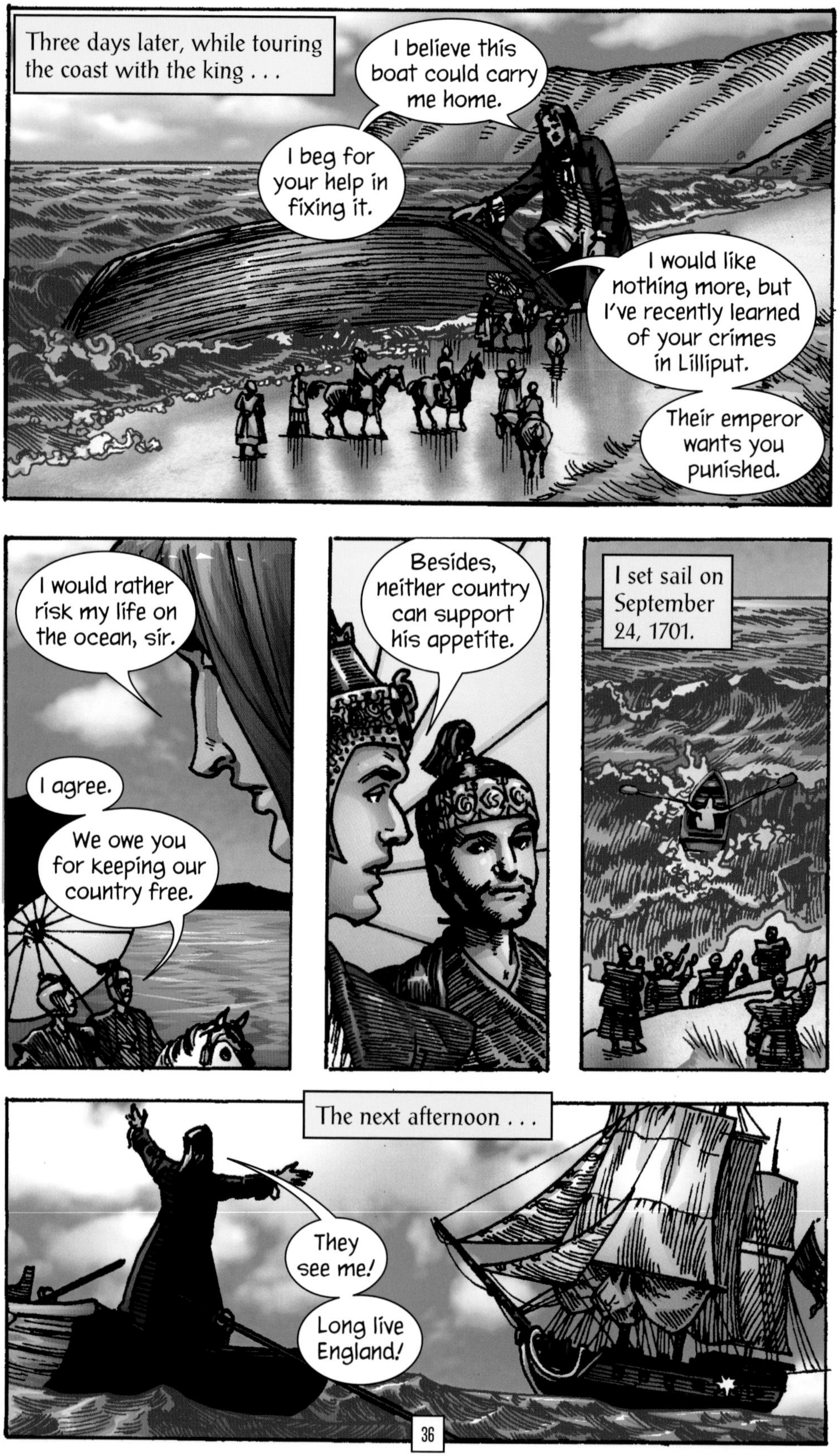
Three days later, while touring the coast with the king . . .
I believe this boat could carry me home.
I beg for your help in fixing it.
I would like nothing more, but I've recently learned of your crimes in Lilliput.
Their emperor wants you punished.
I would rather risk my life on the ocean, sir.
I agree.
We owe you for keeping our country free.
Besides, neither country can support his appetite.
I set sail on September 24, 1701.
The next afternoon . . .
They see me!
Long live England!

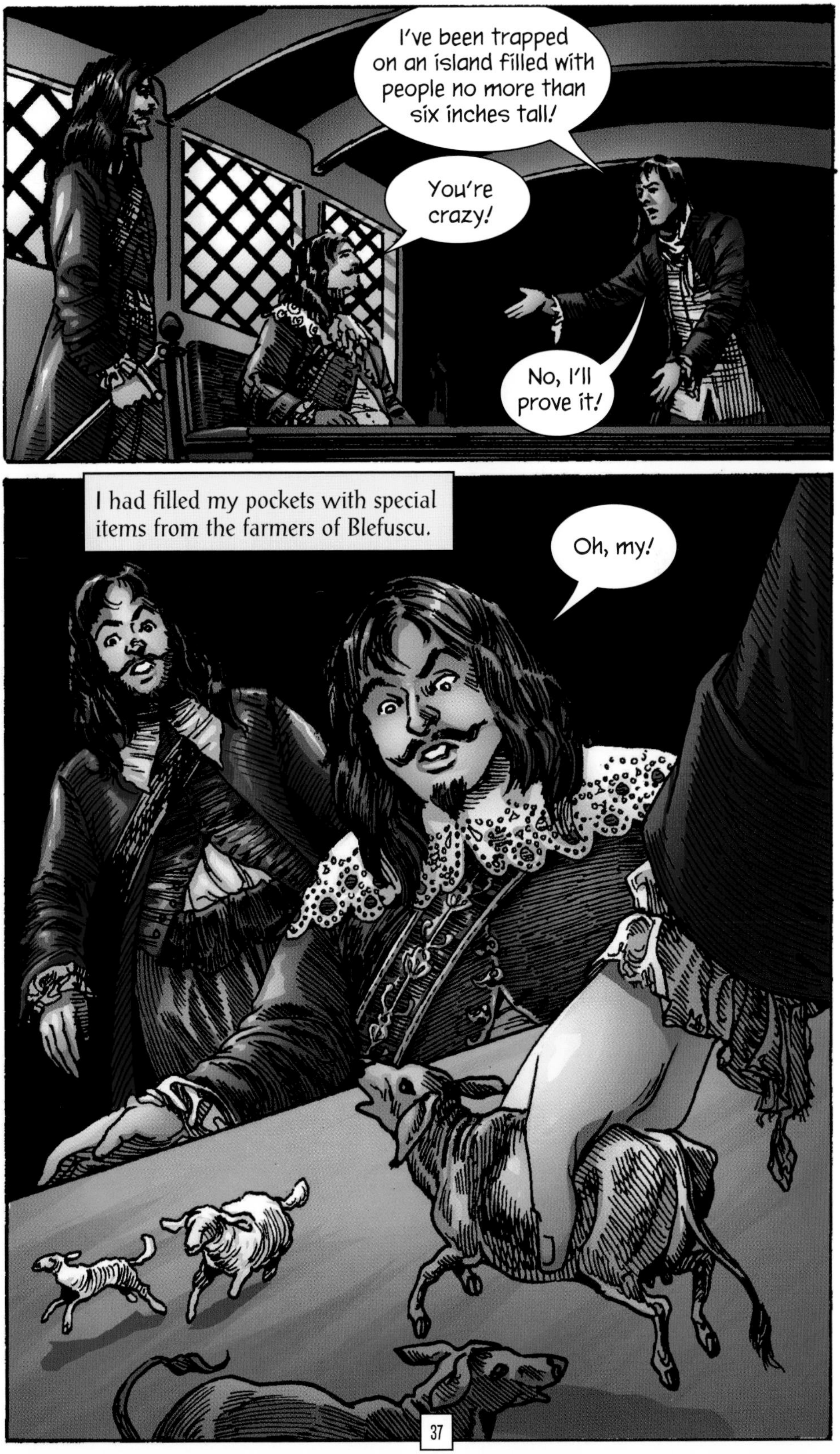
I've been trapped on an island filled with people no more than six inches tall!
You're crazy!
No, I'll prove it!
I had filled my pockets with special items from the farmers of Blefuscu.
Oh, my!

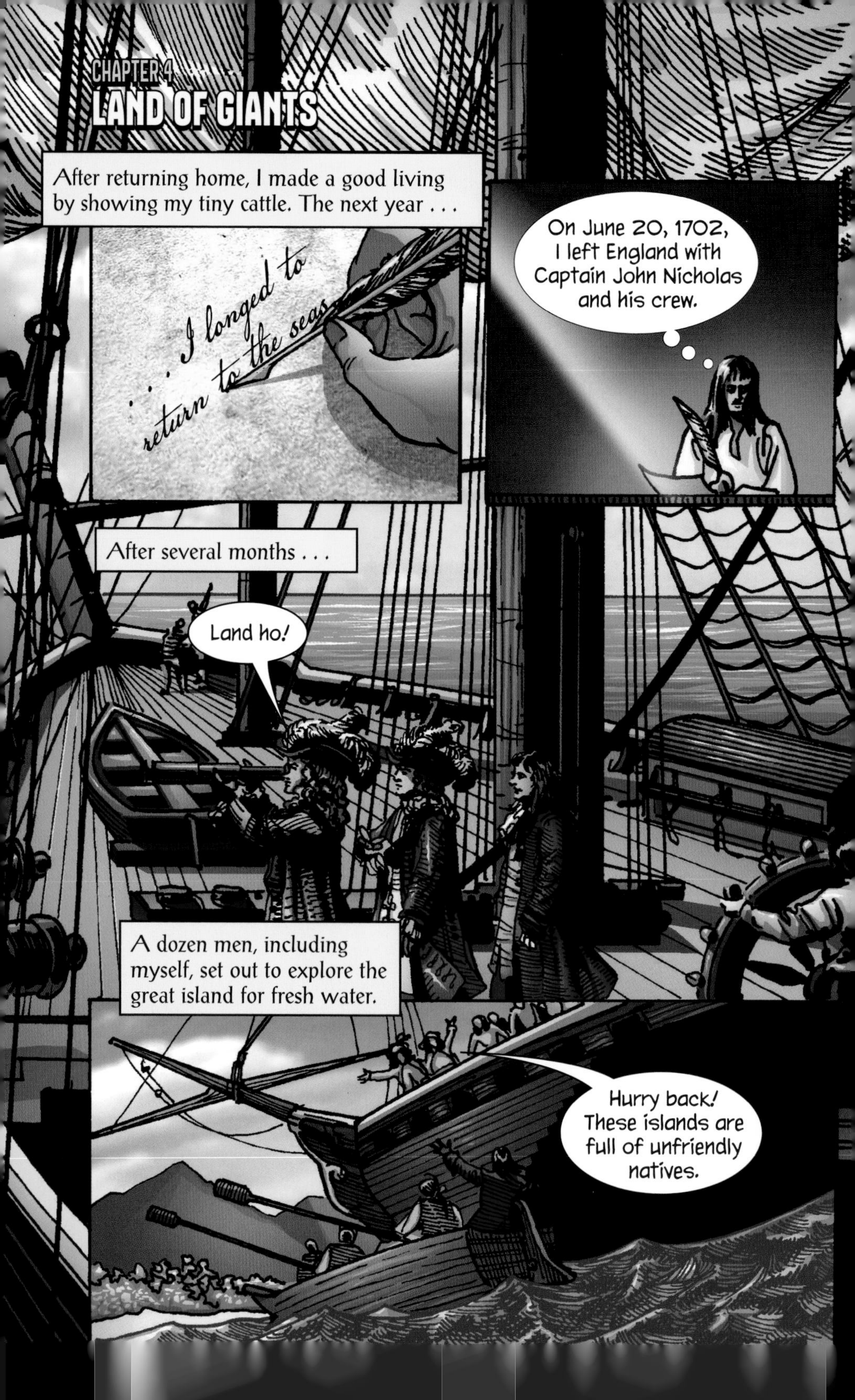
CHAPTER 4
LAND OF GIANTS
After returning home, I made a good living by showing my tiny cattle. The next year . . .
. . . I longed to return to the seas
On June 20, 1702, I left England with Captain John Nicholas and his crew.
After several months . . .
Land ho!
A dozen men, including myself, set out to explore the great island for fresh water.
Hurry back! These islands are full of unfriendly natives.

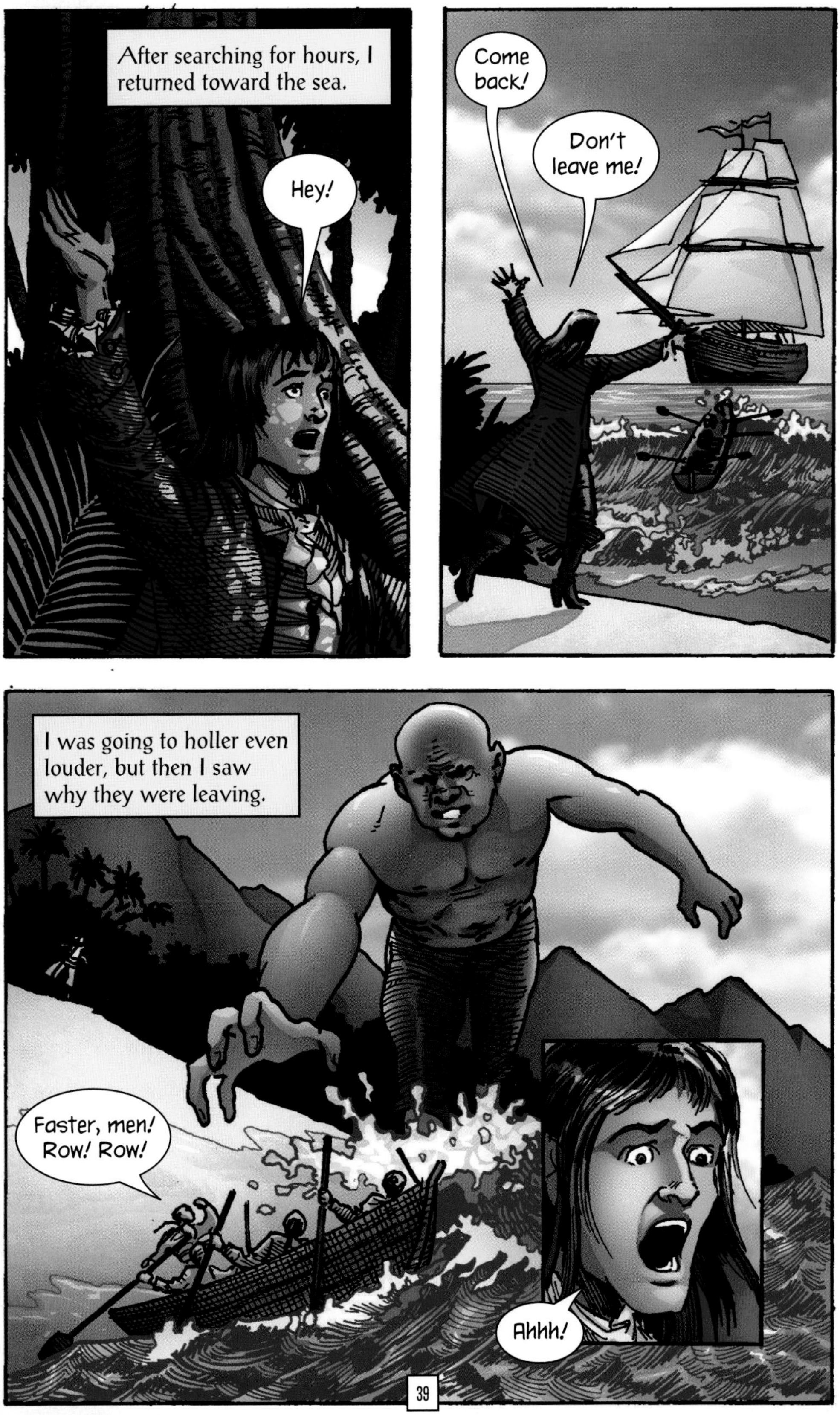
After searching for hours, I returned toward the sea.
Hey!
Come back!
Don't leave me!
I was going to holler even louder, but then I saw why they were leaving.
Faster, men! Row! Row!
Ahhh!

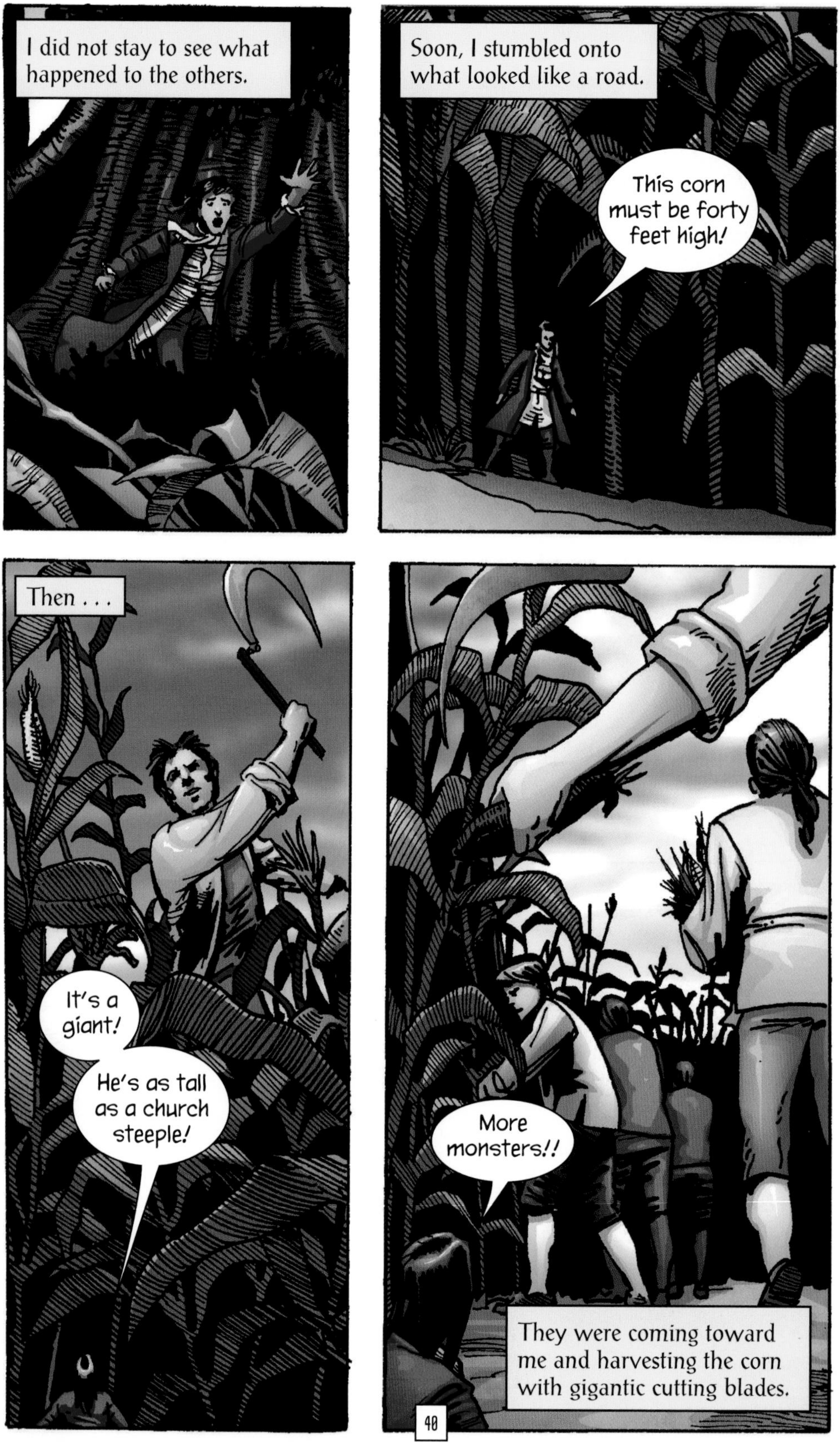
I did not stay to see what happened to the others.
Soon, I stumbled onto what looked like a road.
This corn must be forty feet high!
Then . . .
It's a giant!
He's as tall as a church steeple!
More monsters!!
They were coming toward me and harvesting the corn with gigantic cutting blades.

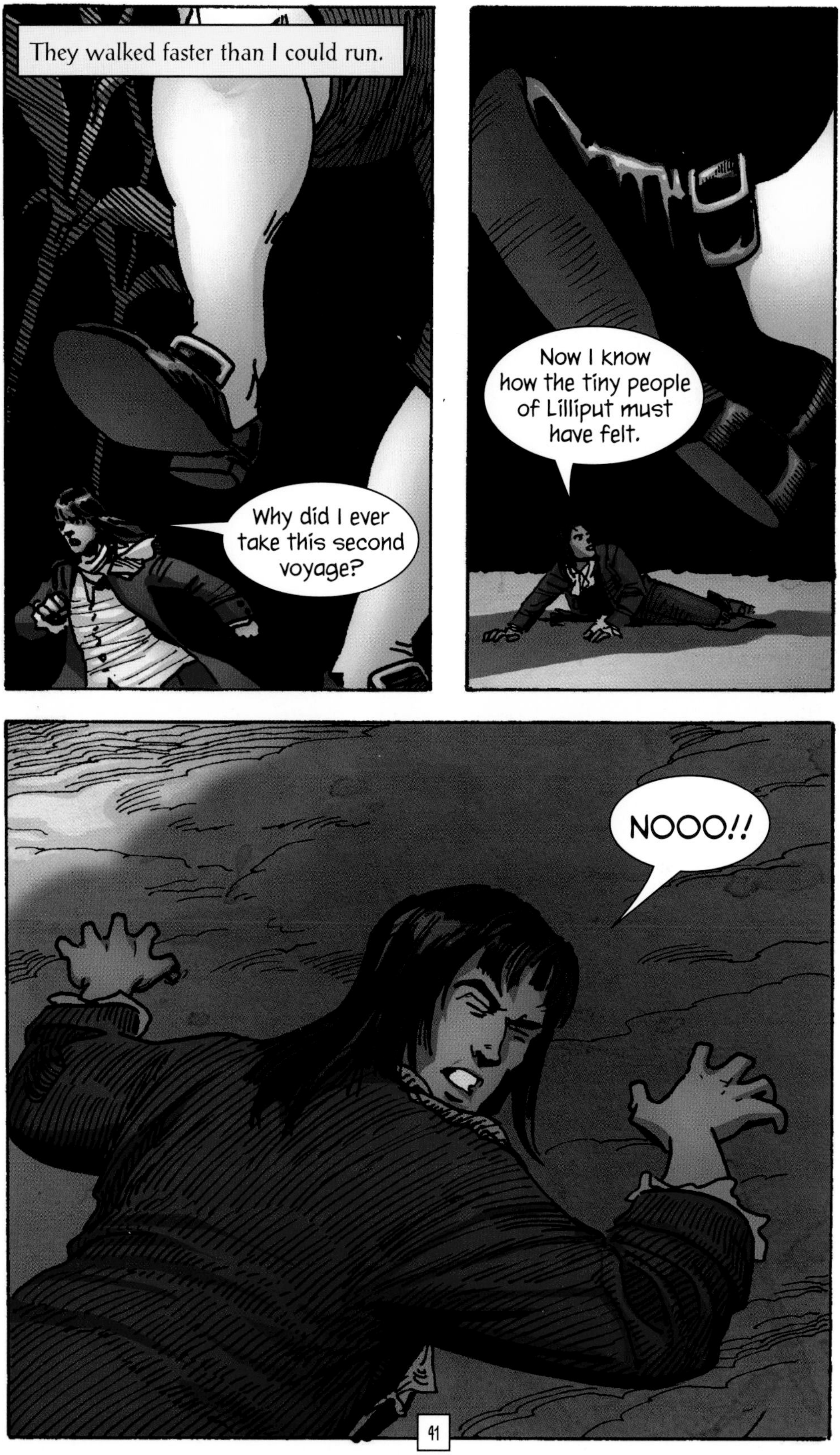
They walked faster than I could run.
Why did I ever take this second voyage?
Now I know how the tiny people of Lilliput must have felt.
NOOO!!

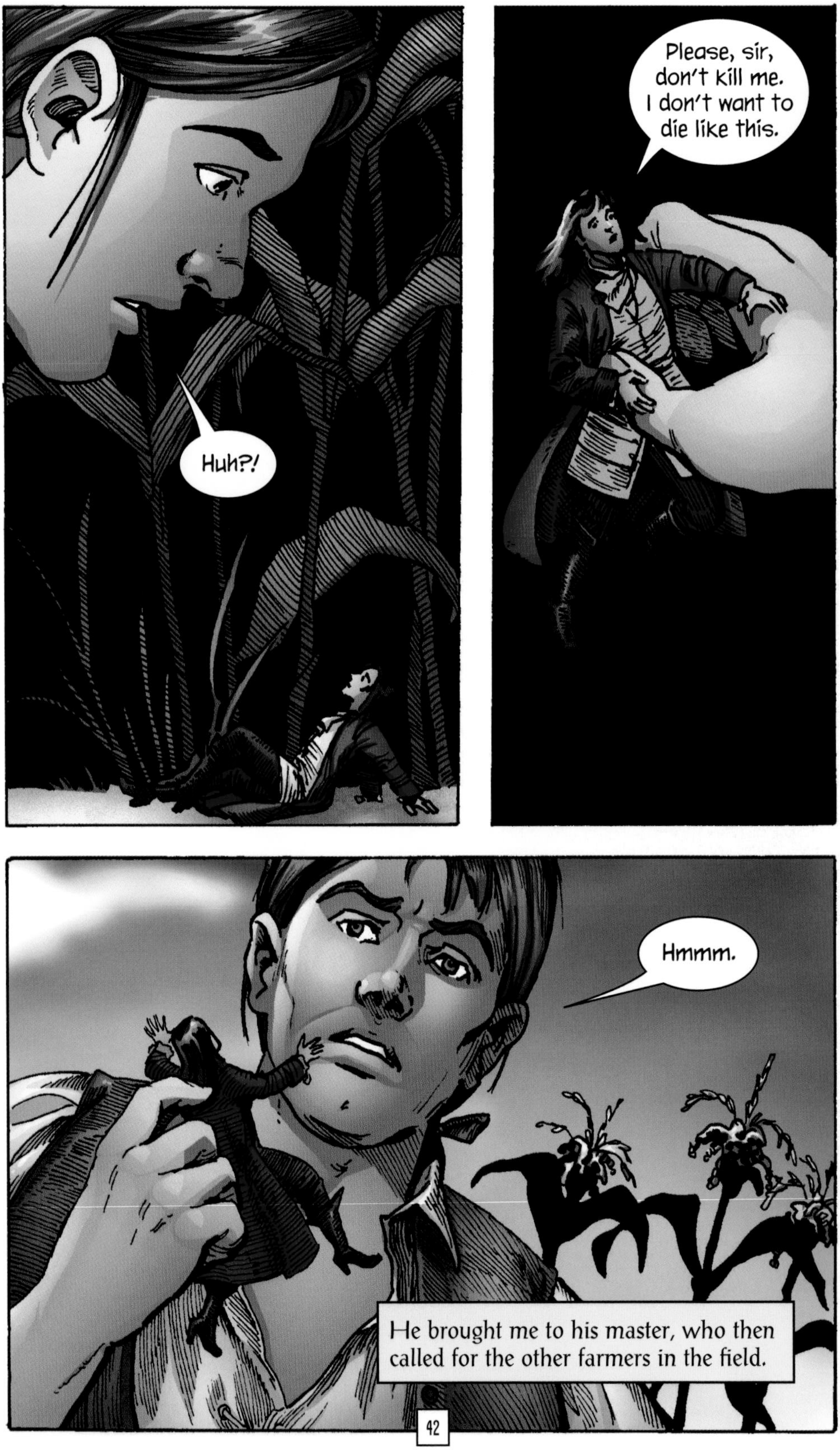
Huh?!
Please, sir, don't kill me. I don't want to die like this.
Hmmm.
He brought me to his master, who then called for the other farmers in the field.

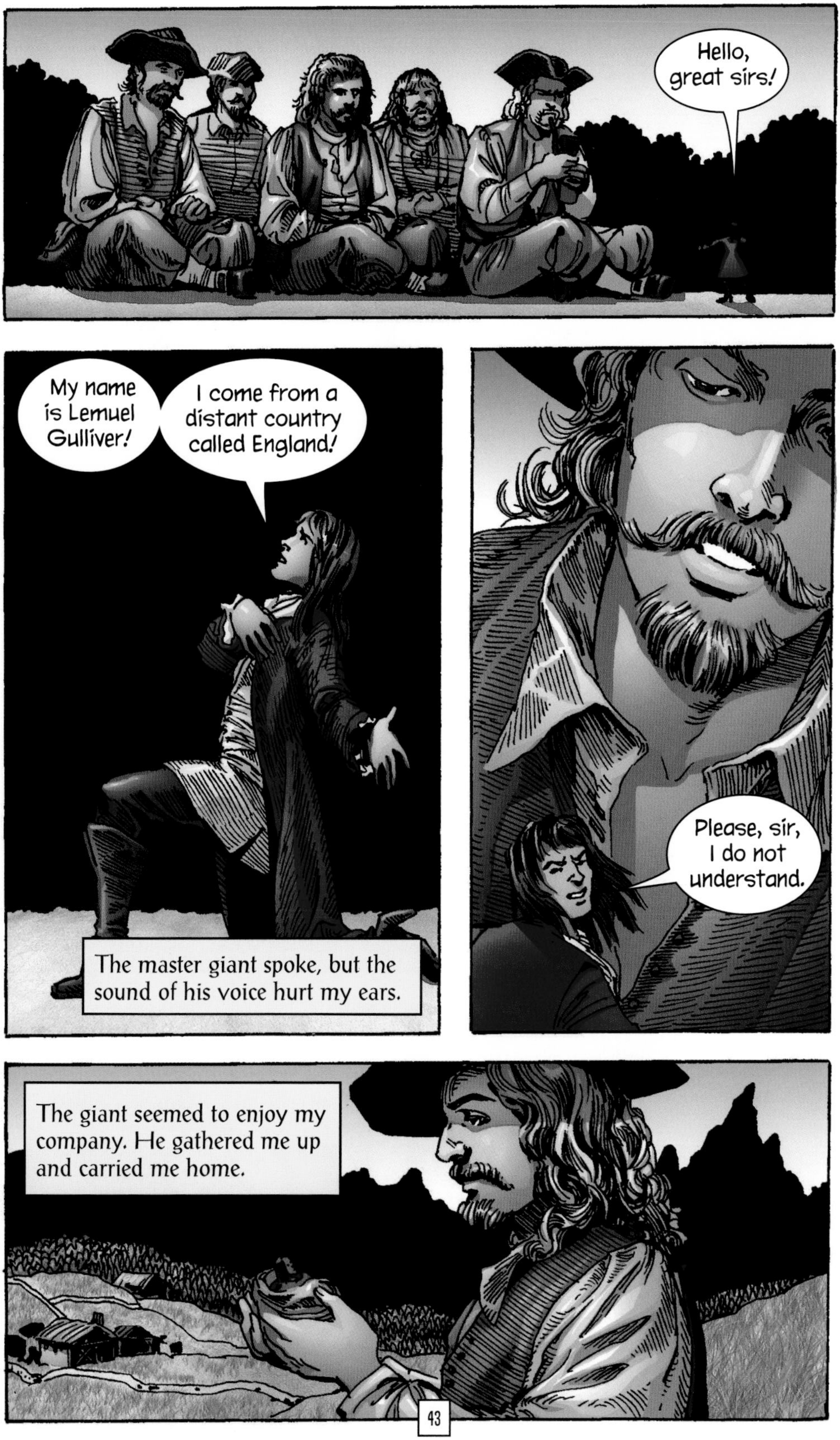
Hello, great sirs!
My name is Lemuel Gulliver!
I come from a distant country called England!
The master giant spoke, but the sound of his voice hurt my ears.
Please, sir, I do not understand.
The giant seemed to enjoy my company. He gathered me up and carried me home.

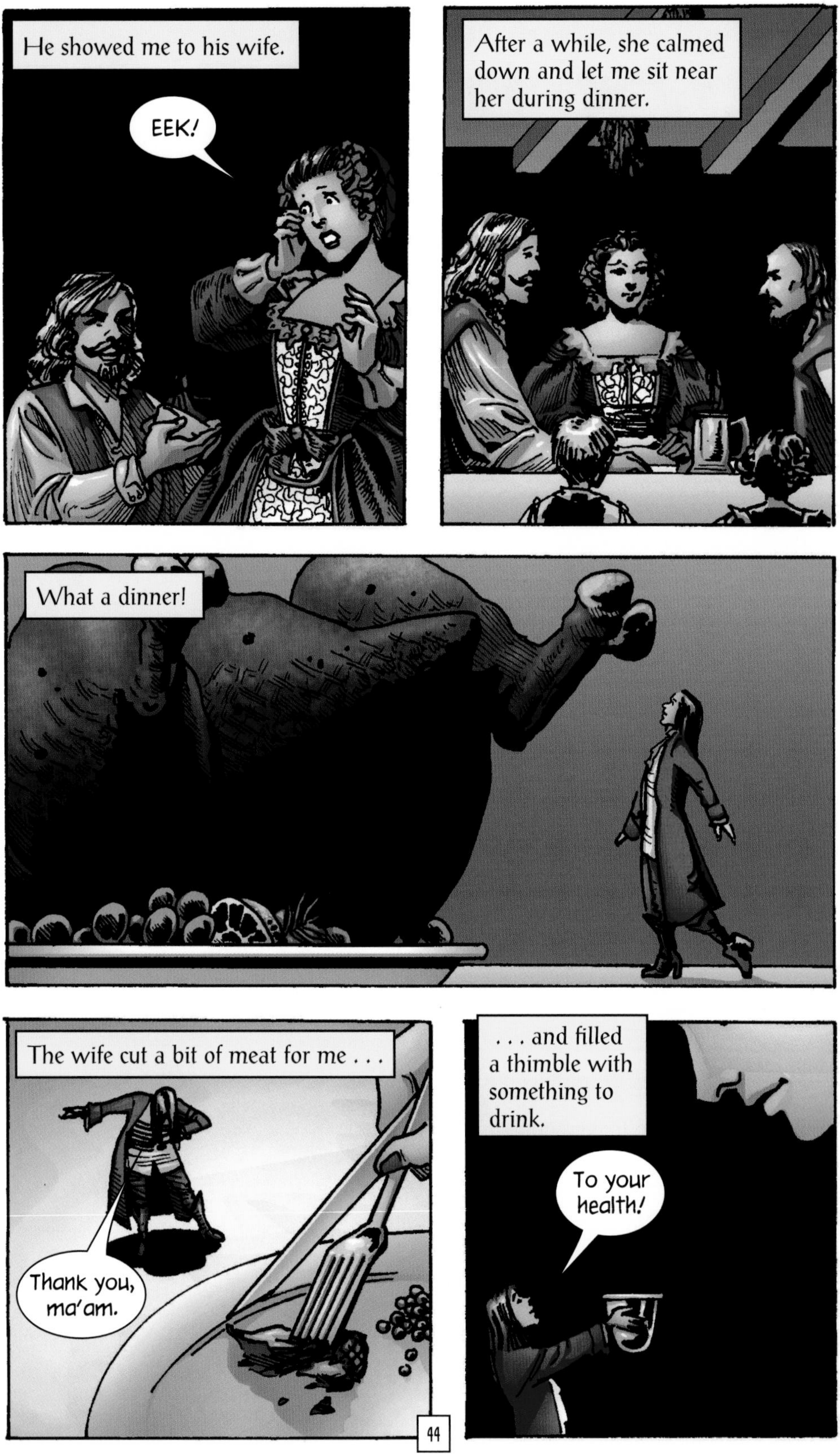
He showed me to his wife.
EEK!
After a while, she calmed down and let me sit near her during dinner.
What a dinner!
The wife cut a bit of meat for me . . .
Thank you, ma'am.
. . . and filled a thimble with something to drink.
To your health!

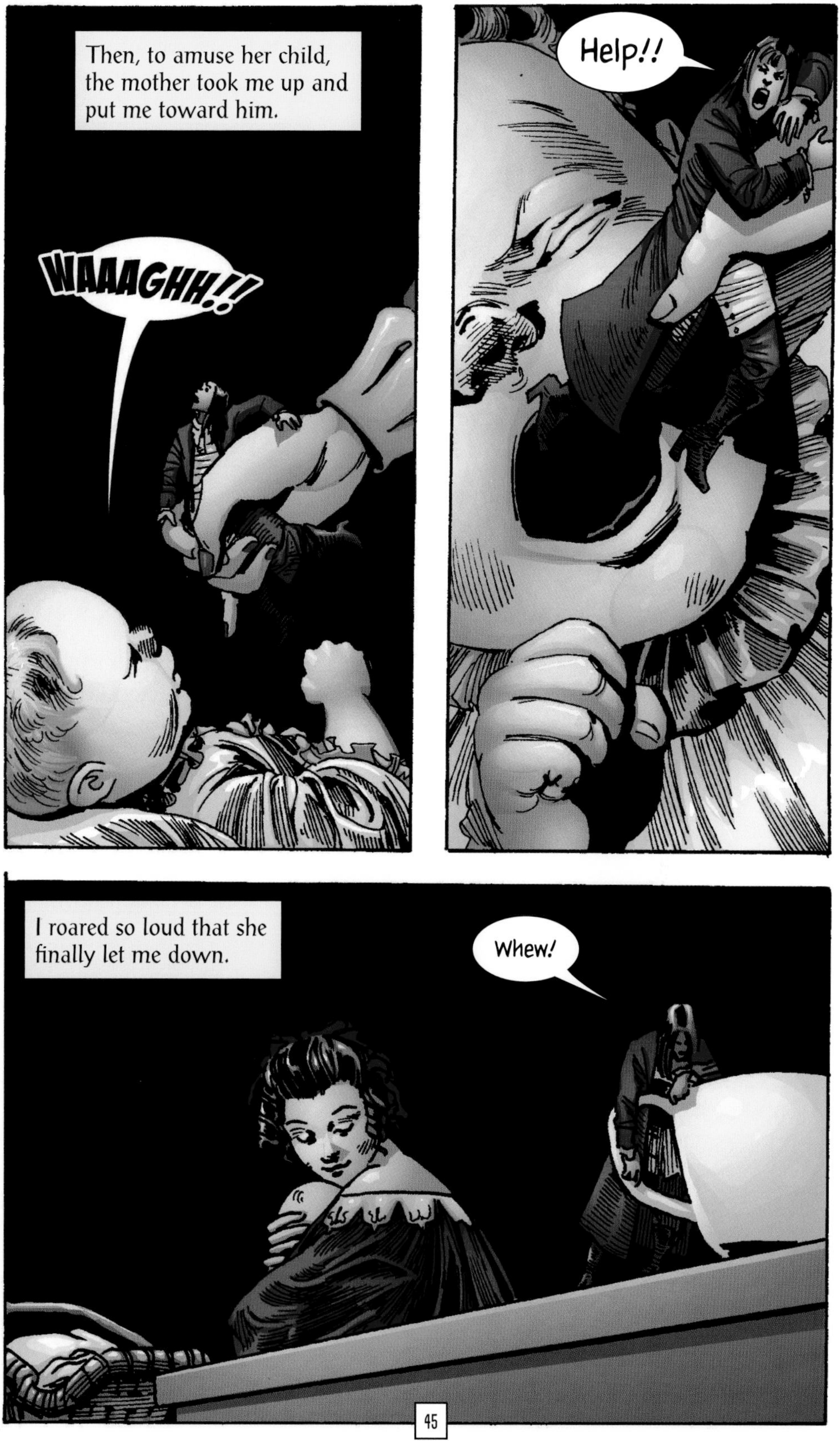
Then, to amuse her child, the mother took me up and put me toward him.
WAAAGHH!!
Help!!
I roared so loud that she finally let me down.
Whew!

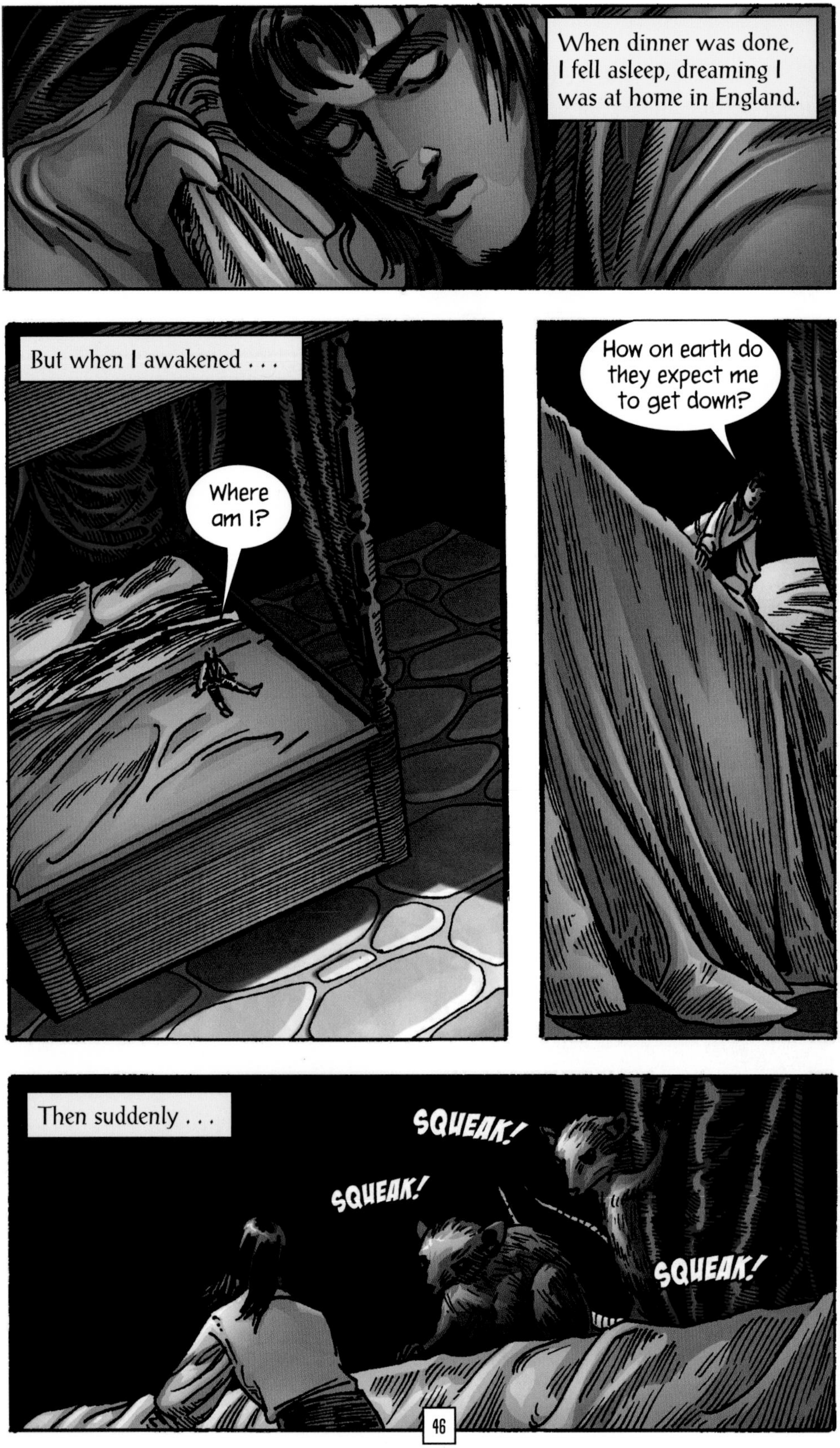
When dinner was done, I fell asleep, dreaming I was at home in England.
But when I awakened . . .
Where am I?
How on earth do they expect me to get down?
Then suddenly . . .
SQUEAK!
SQUEAK!
SQUEAK!

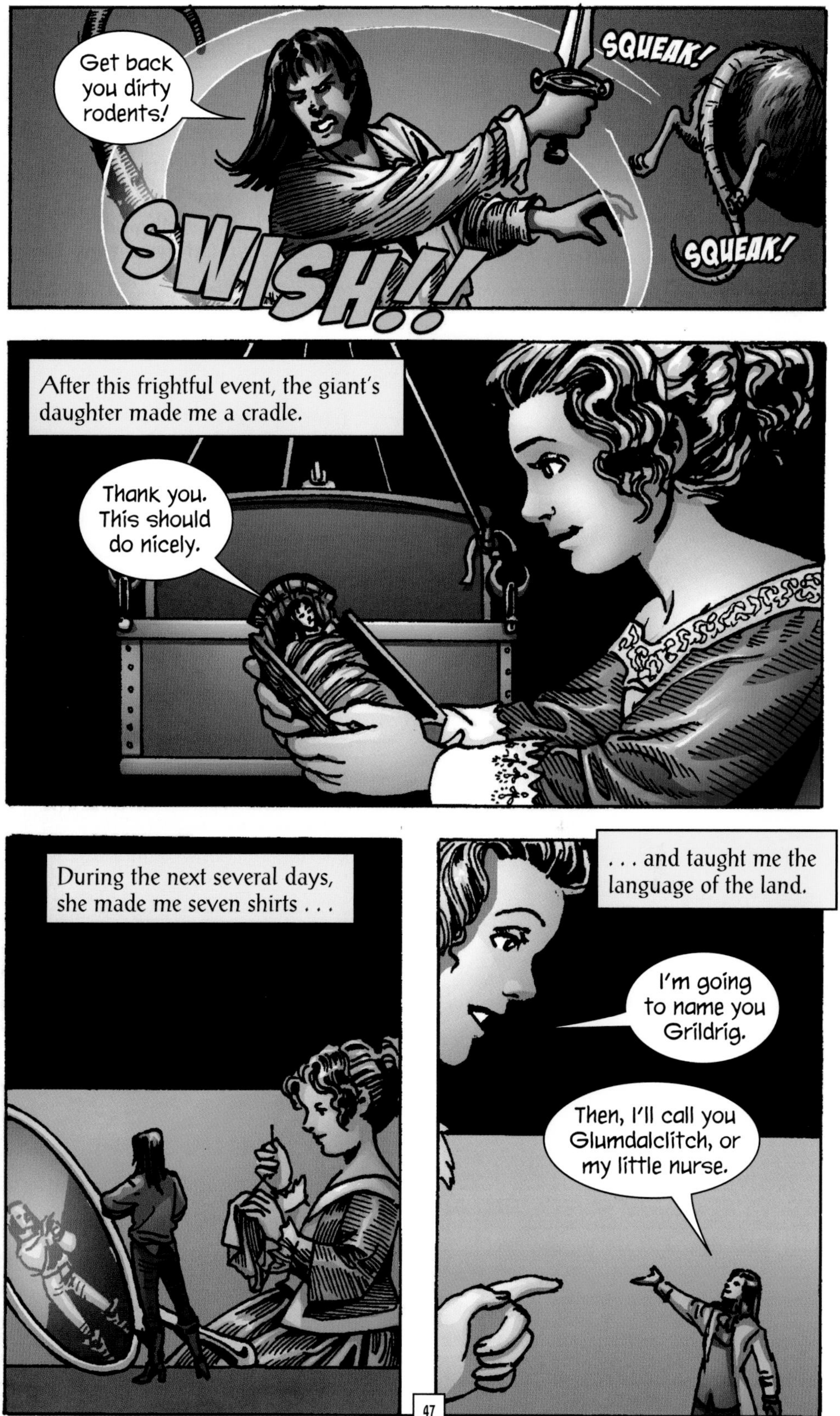

Get back you dirty rodents!
SQUEAK!
SWISH!!
SQUEAK!
After this frightful event, the giant's daughter made me a cradle.
Thank you. This should do nicely.
During the next several days, she made me seven shirts . . .
. . . and taught me the language of the land.
I'm going to name you Grildrig.
Then, I'll call you Glumdalclitch, or my little nurse.

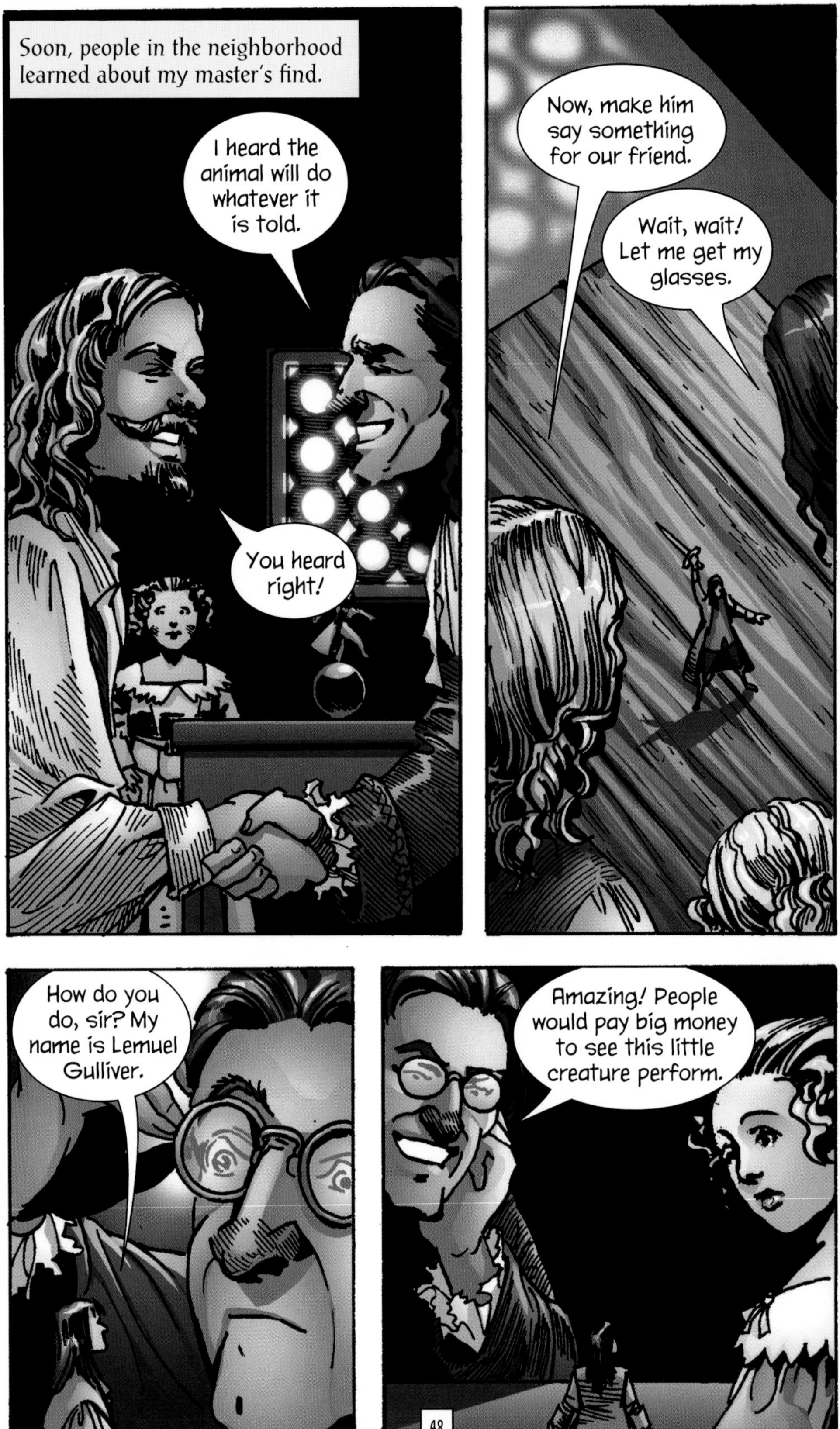
Soon, people in the neighborhood learned about my master's find.
I heard the animal will do whatever it is told.
You heard right!
Now, make him say something for our friend.
Wait, wait! Let me get my glasses.
How do you do, sir? My name is Lemuel Gulliver.
Amazing! People would pay big money to see this little creature perform.

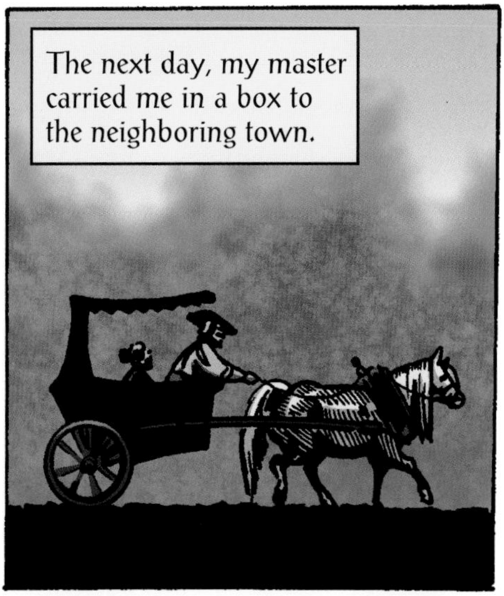
The next day, my master carried me in a box to the neighboring town.

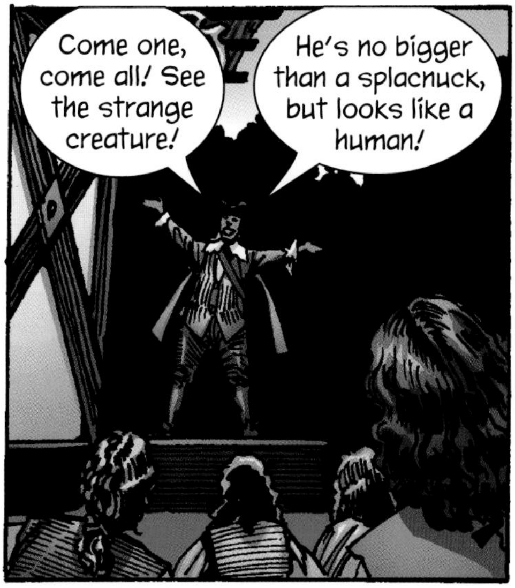
Come one, come all! See the strange creature!
He's no bigger than a splacnuck, but looks like a human!

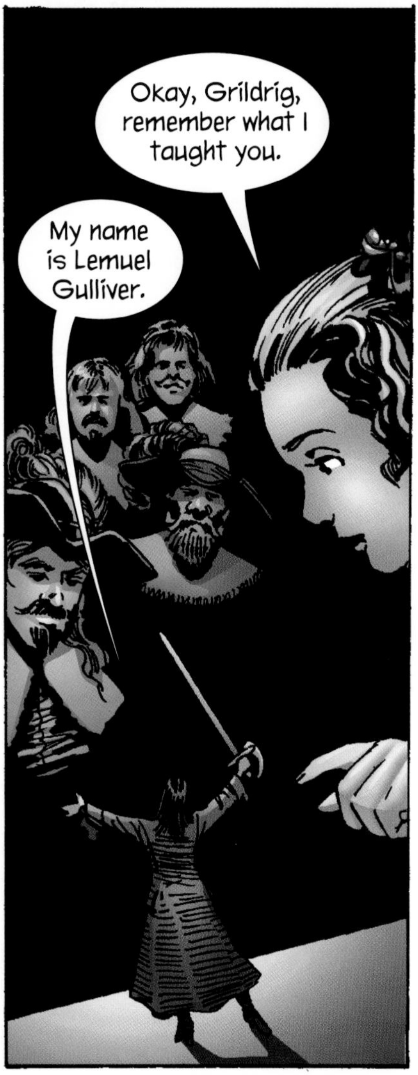
Okay, Grildrig, remember what I taught you.
My name is Lemuel Gulliver.

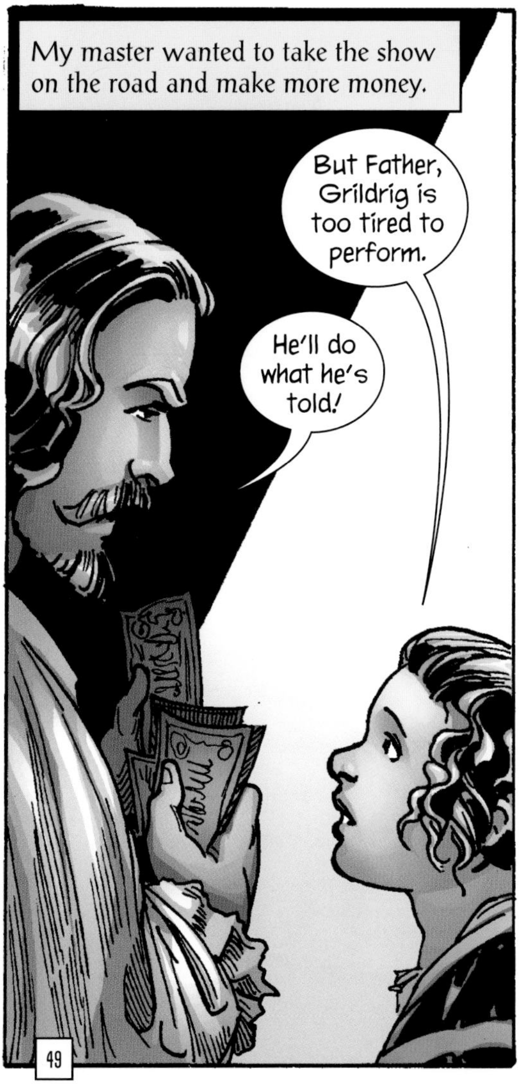
My master wanted to take the show on the road and make more money.
But Father, Grildrig is too tired to perform.
He'll do what he's told!

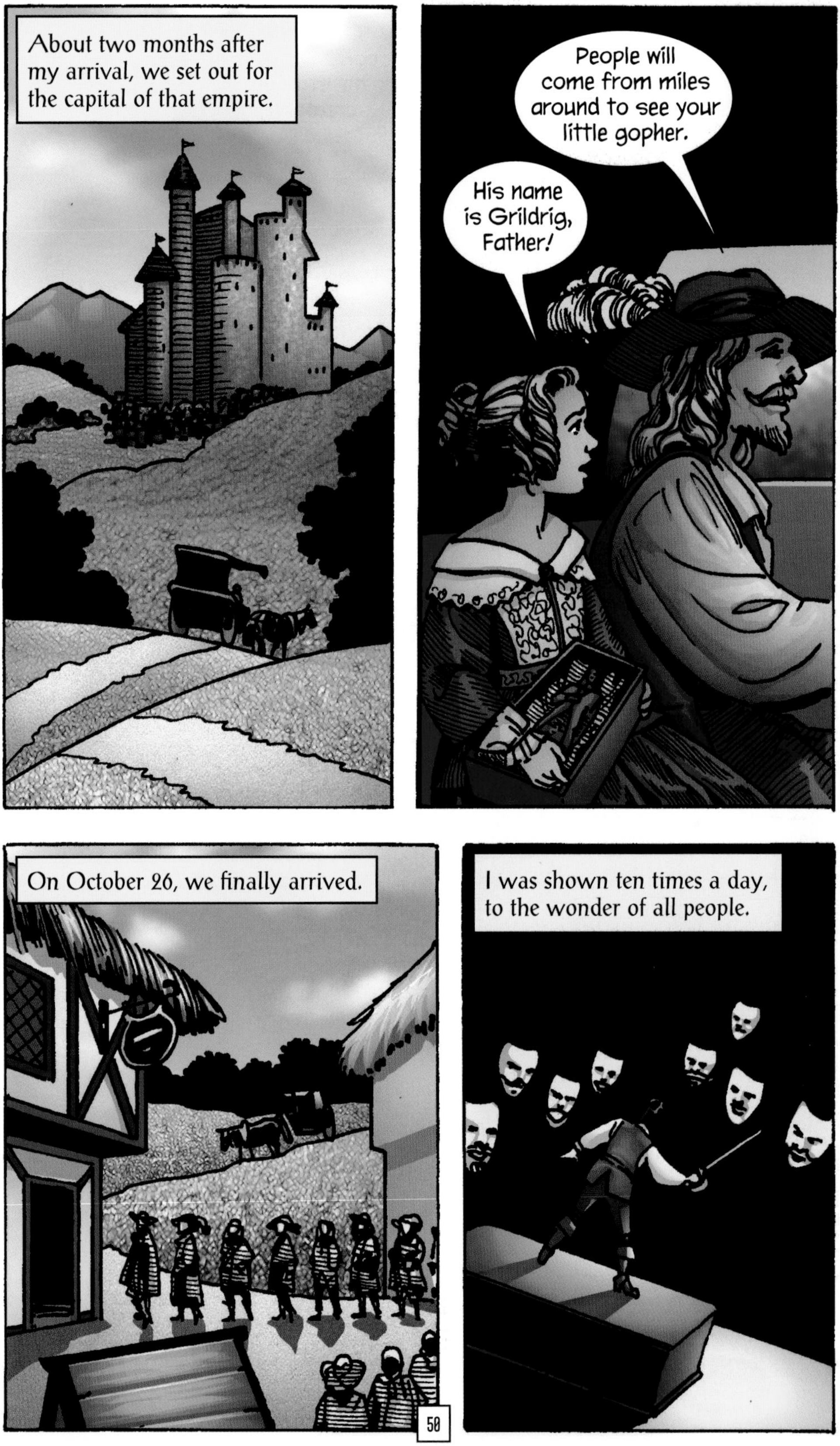
About two months after my arrival, we set out for the capital of that empire.
People will come from miles around to see your little gopher.
His name is Grildrig, Father!
On October 26, we finally arrived.
I was shown ten times a day, to the wonder of all people.

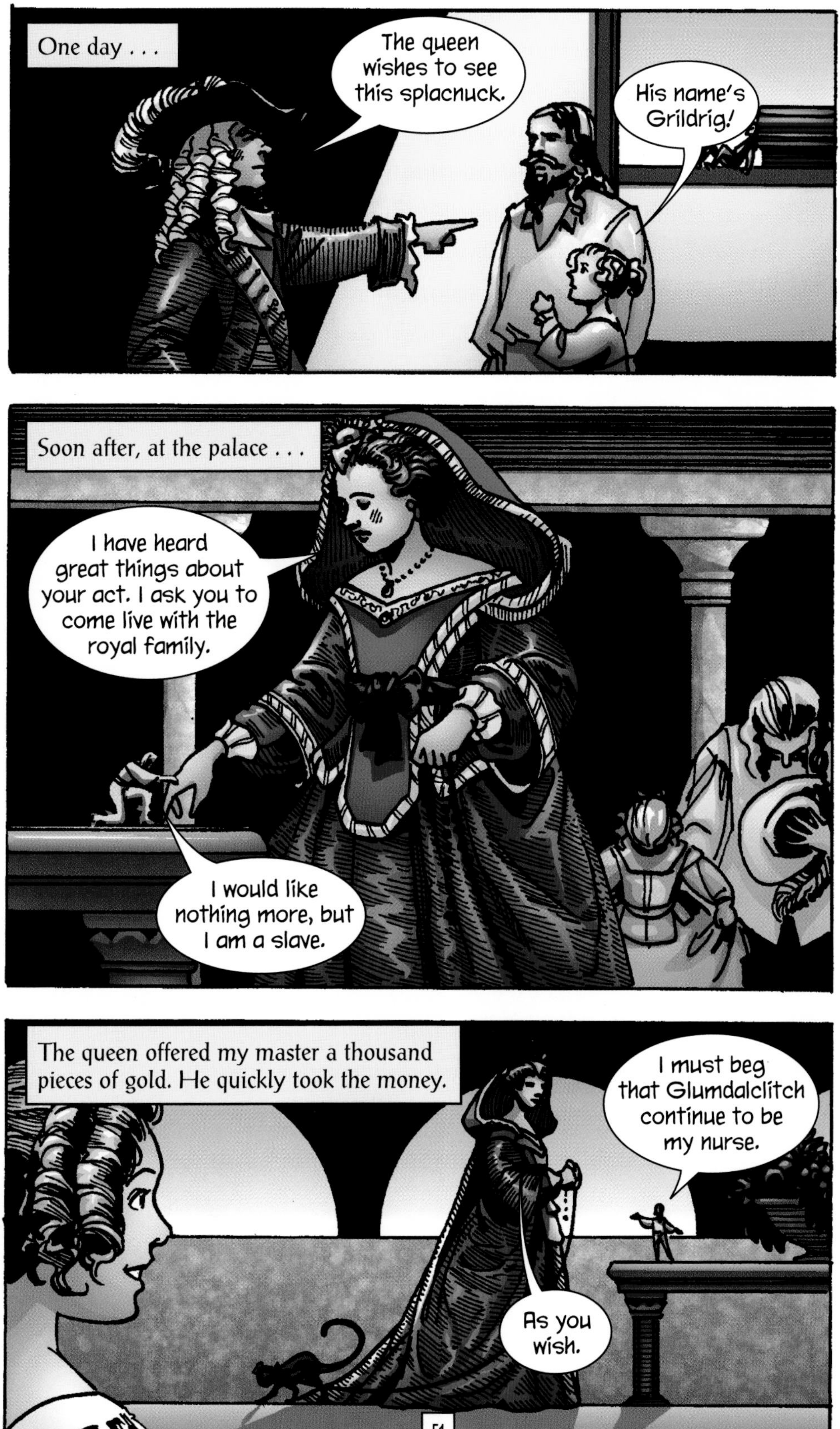
One day . . .
The queen wishes to see this splacnuck.
His name's Grildrig!
Soon after, at the palace . . .
I have heard great things about your act. I ask you to come live with the royal family.
I would like nothing more, but I am a slave.
The queen offered my master a thousand pieces of gold. He quickly took the money.
I must beg that Glumdalclitch continue to be my nurse.
As you wish.

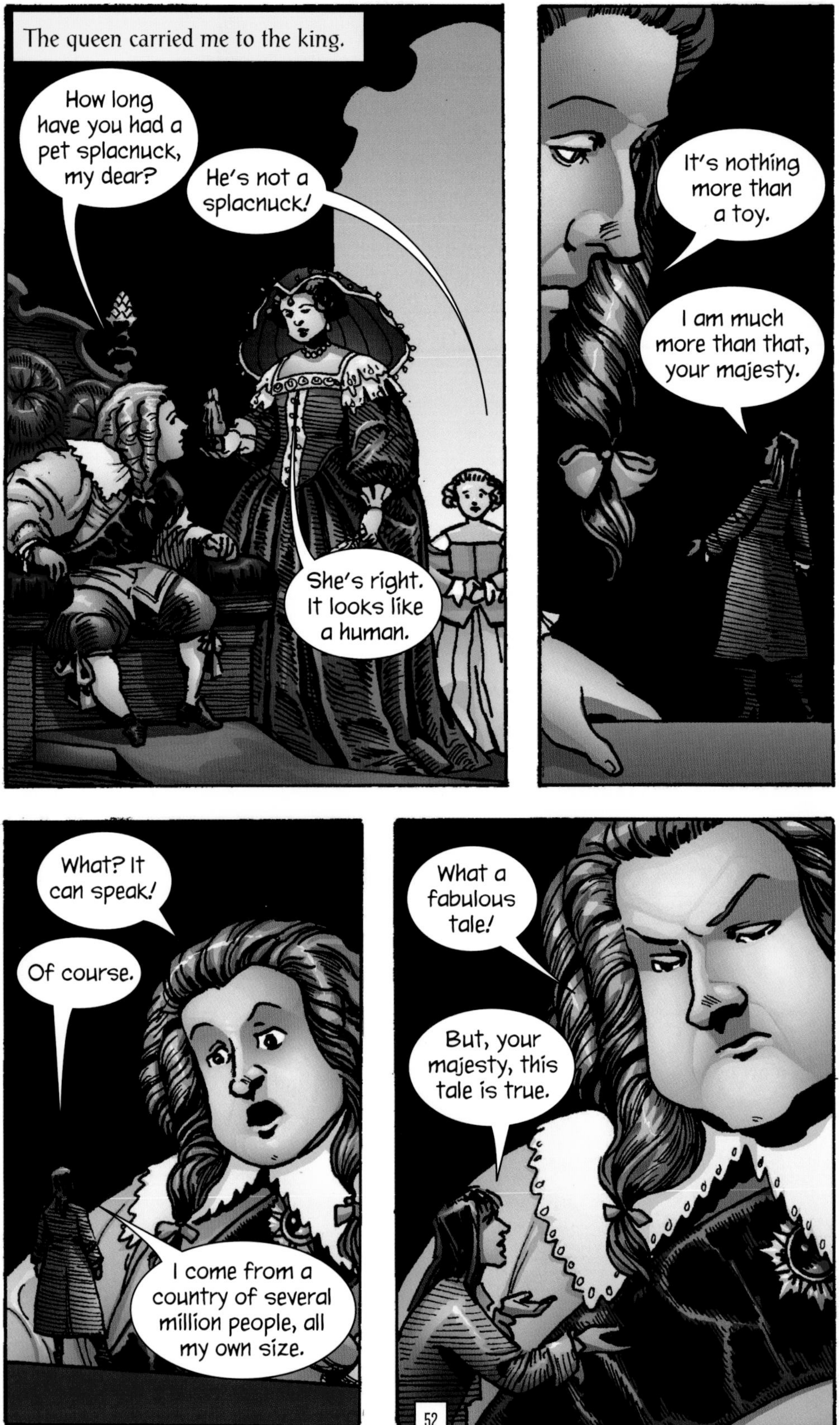
The queen carried me to the king.
How long have you had a pet splacnuck, my dear?
He's not a splacnuck!
She's right. It looks like a human.
It's nothing more than a toy.
I am much more than that, your majesty.
What? It can speak!
Of course.
I come from a country of several million people, all my own size.
What a fabulous tale!
But, your majesty, this tale is true.

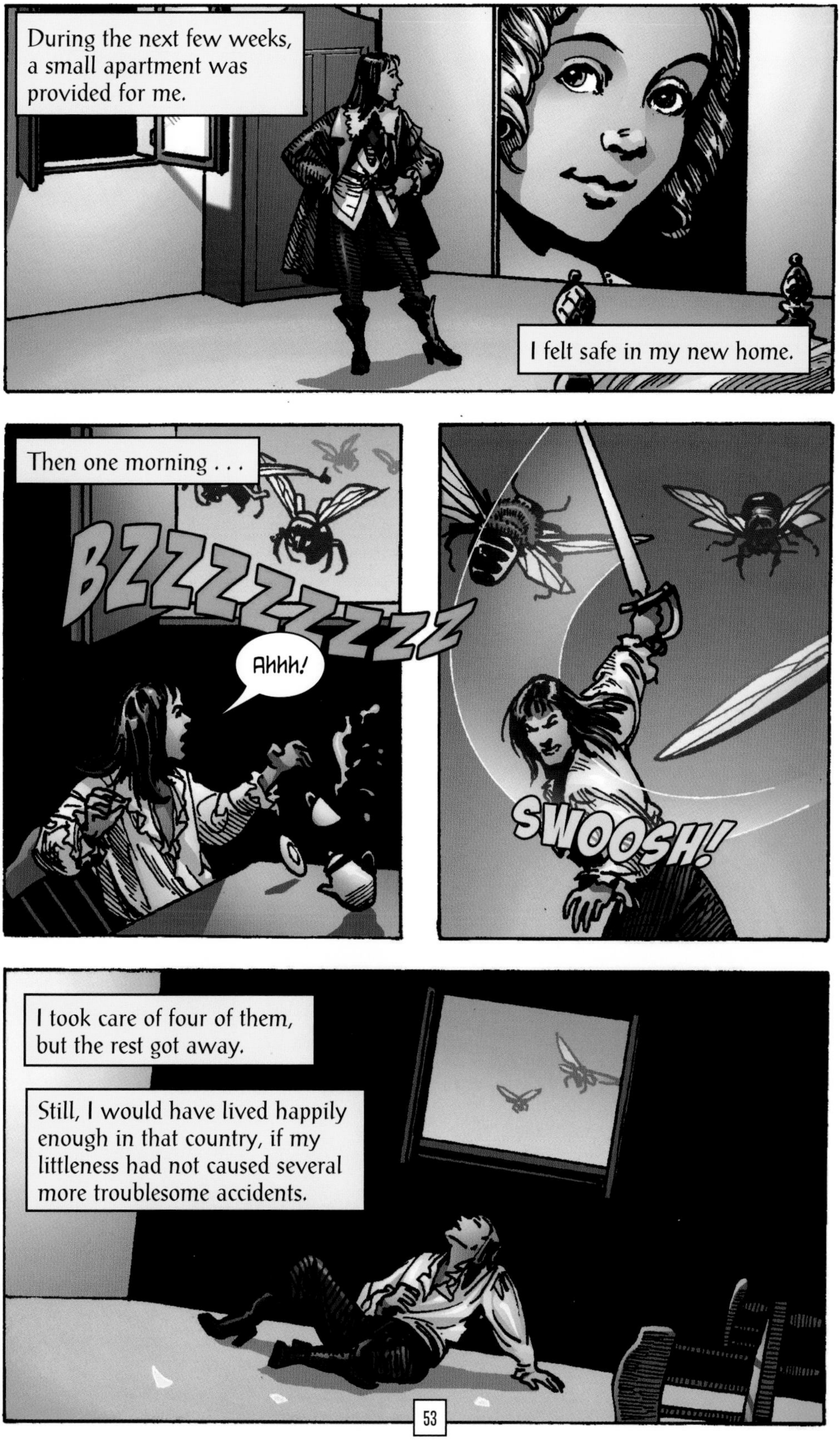
During the next few weeks, a small apartment was provided for me.
I felt safe in my new home.
Then one morning . . .
BZZZZZZZZZ
Ahhh!
SWOOSH!
I took care of four of them, but the rest got away.
Still, I would have lived happily enough in that country, if my littleness had not caused several more troublesome accidents.

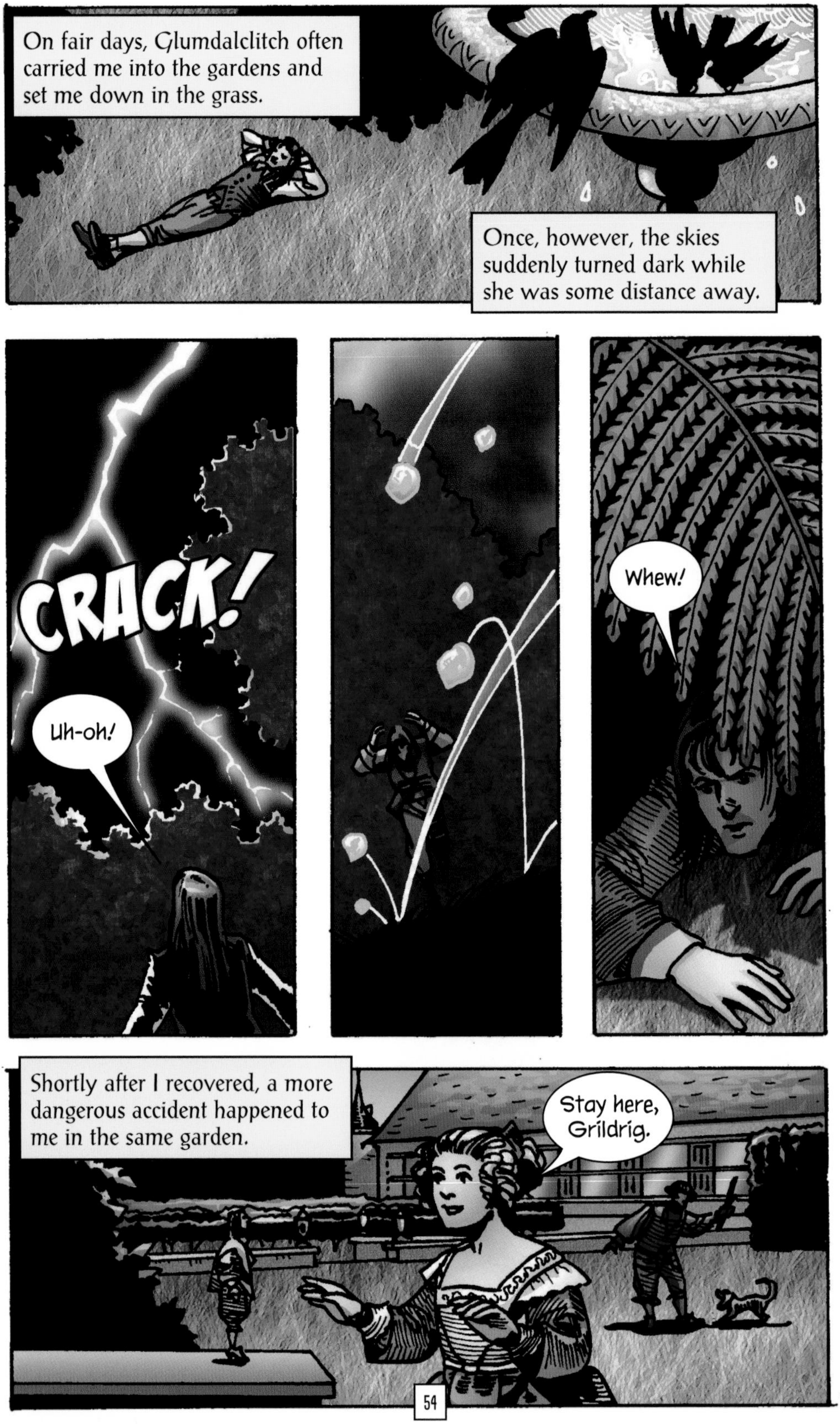
On fair days, Glumdalclitch often carried me into the gardens and set me down in the grass.
Once, however, the skies suddenly turned dark while she was some distance away.
CRACK!
Uh-oh!
Whew!
Shortly after I recovered, a more dangerous accident happened to me in the same garden.
Stay here, Grildrig.

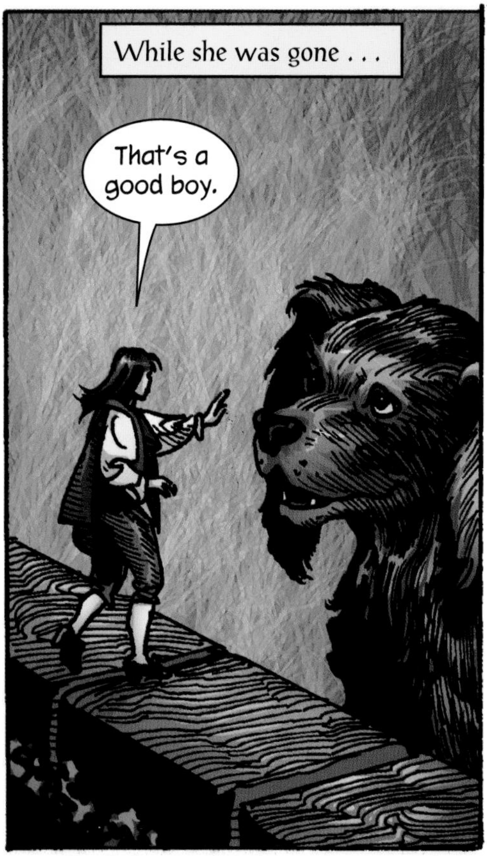
While she was gone . . .
That's a good boy.

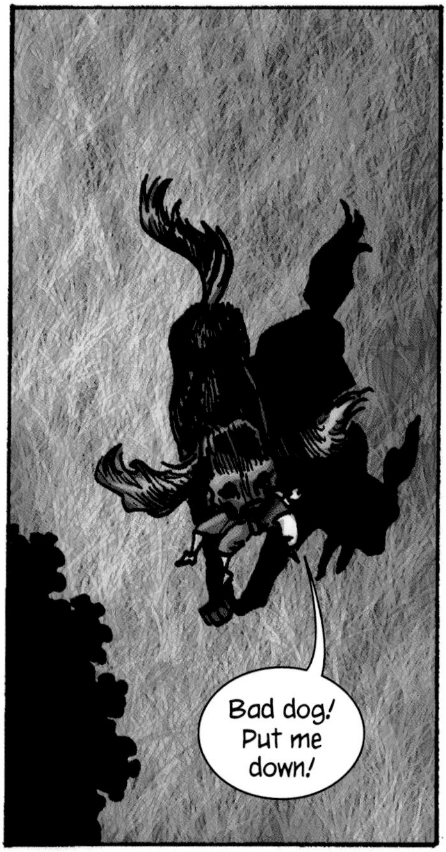
Bad dog! Put me down!

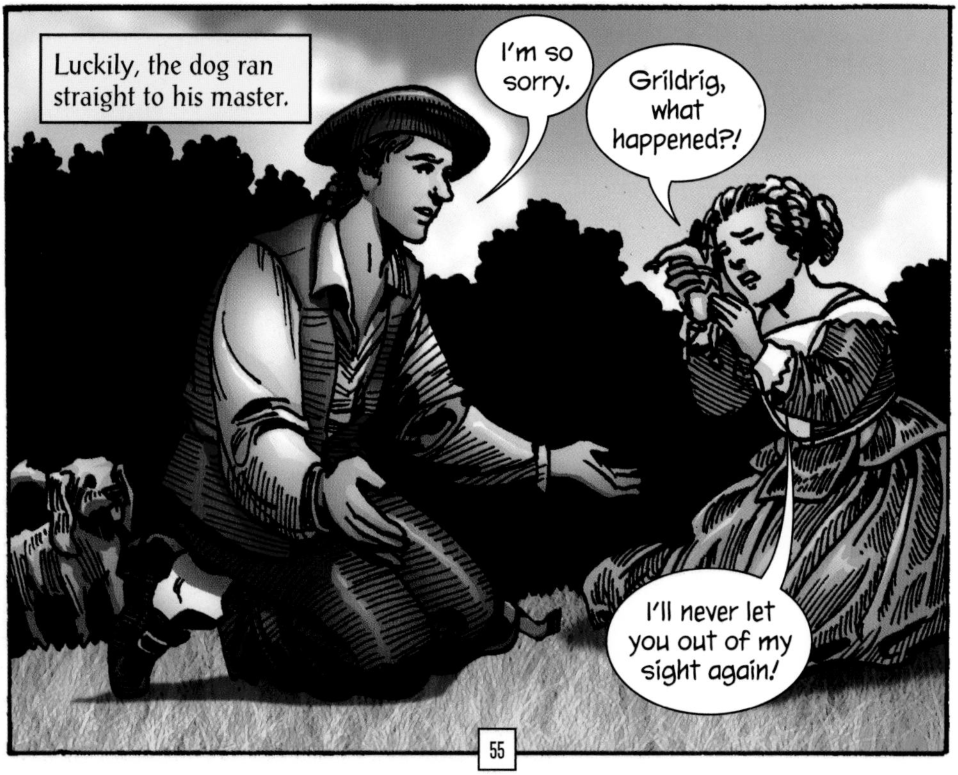
Luckily, the dog ran straight to his master.
I'm so sorry.
Grildrig, what happened?!
I'll never let you out of my sight again!

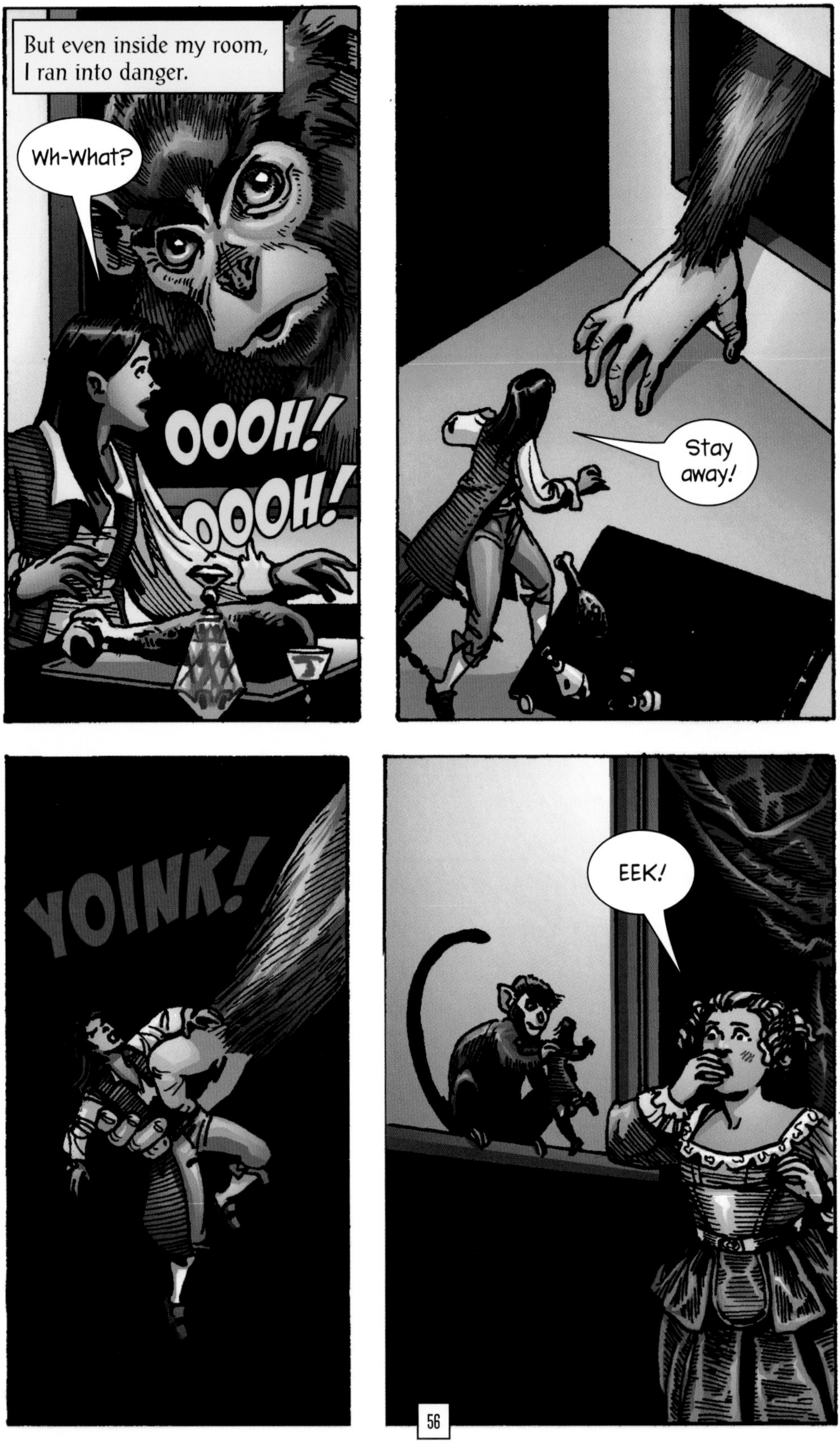
But even inside my room, I ran into danger.
Wh-What?
OOOH! OOOH!
Stay away!
YOINK!
EEK!

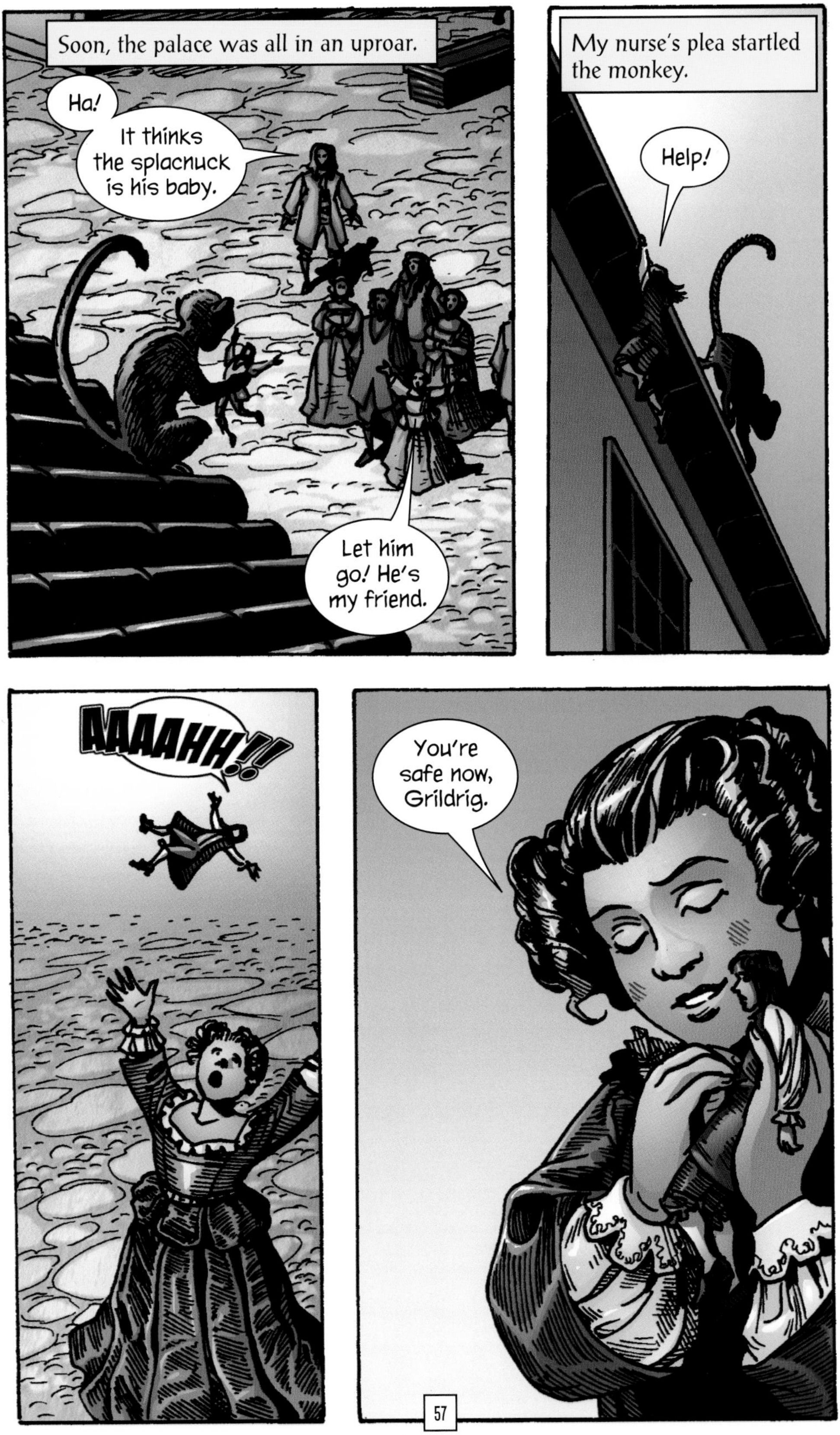

Soon, the palace was all in an uproar.
Ha!
It thinks the splacnuck is his baby.
Let him go! He's my friend.
My nurse's plea startled the monkey.
Help!
AAAAHH!!
You're safe now, Grildrig.

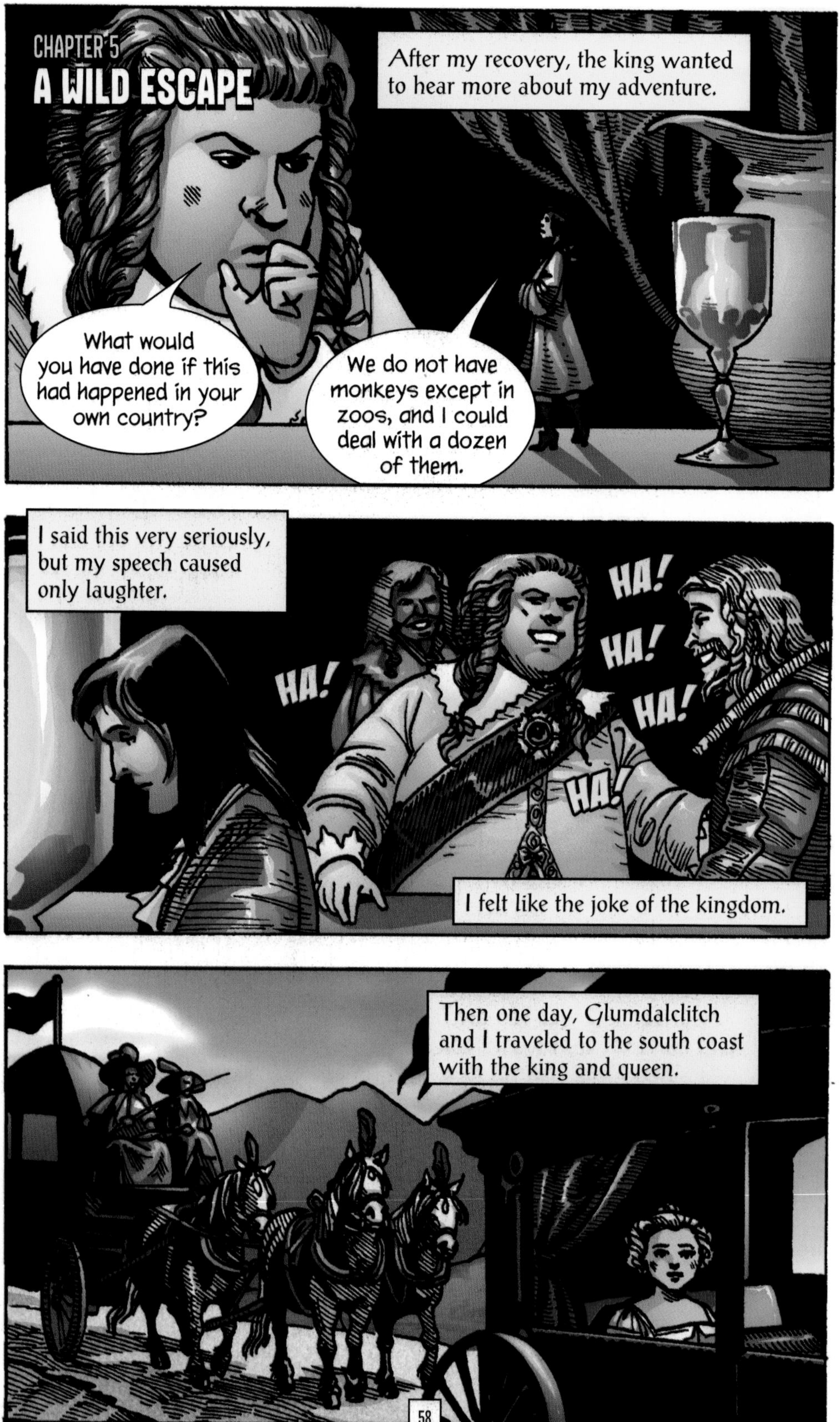
CHAPTER 5
A WILD ESCAPE
After my recovery, the king wanted to hear more about my adventure.
What would you have done if this had happened in your own country?
We do not have monkeys except in zoos, and I could deal with a dozen of them.
I said this very seriously, but my speech caused only laughter.
HA!
HA!
HA!
HA!
HA!
I felt like the joke of the kingdom.
Then one day, Glumdalclitch and I traveled to the south coast with the king and queen.

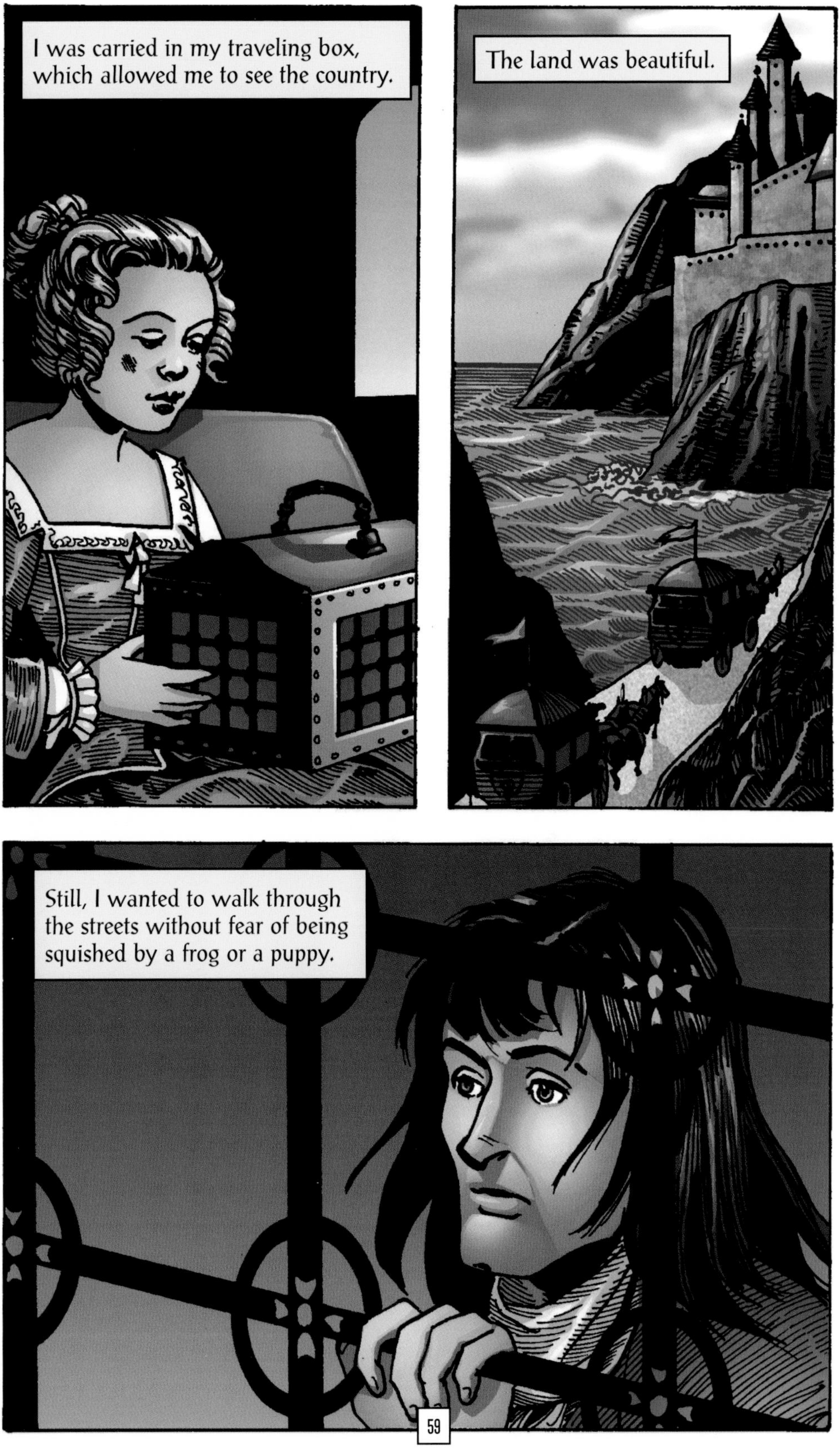
I was carried in my traveling box, which allowed me to see the country.
The land was beautiful.
Still, I wanted to walk through the streets without fear of being squished by a frog or a puppy.

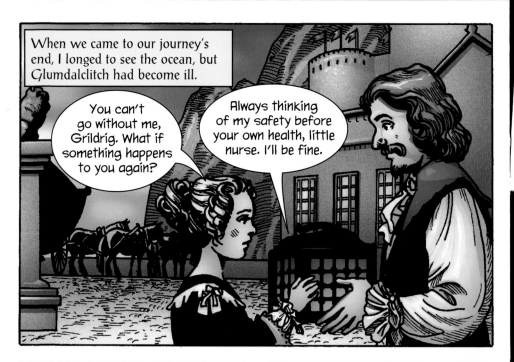

When we came to our journey's end, I longed to see the ocean, but Glumdalclitch had become ill.

You can't go without me, Grildrig. What if something happens to you again?

Always thinking of my safety before your own health, little nurse. I'll be fine.

With Glumdalclitch's permission, a royal servant took me to the seashore about half an hours' walk from the palace.

Oh, how I wish to see my own country.

After a while, I decided to take a short nap inside my traveling closet.

ZZZZZZZZZZZ

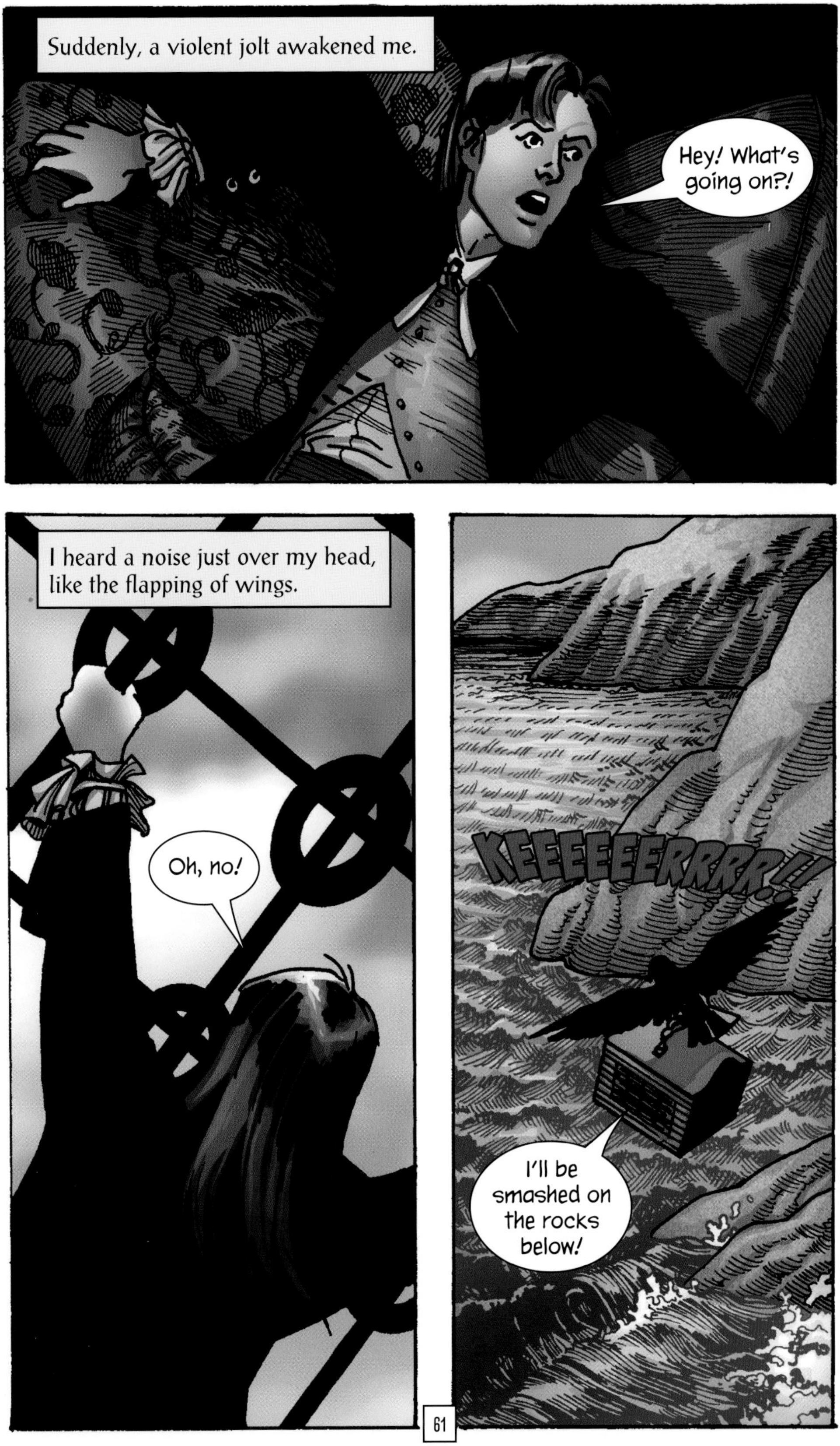
Suddenly, a violent jolt awakened me.
Hey! What's going on?!
I heard a noise just over my head, like the flapping of wings.
Oh, no!
KEEEEEERRRR?!!
I'll be smashed on the rocks below!

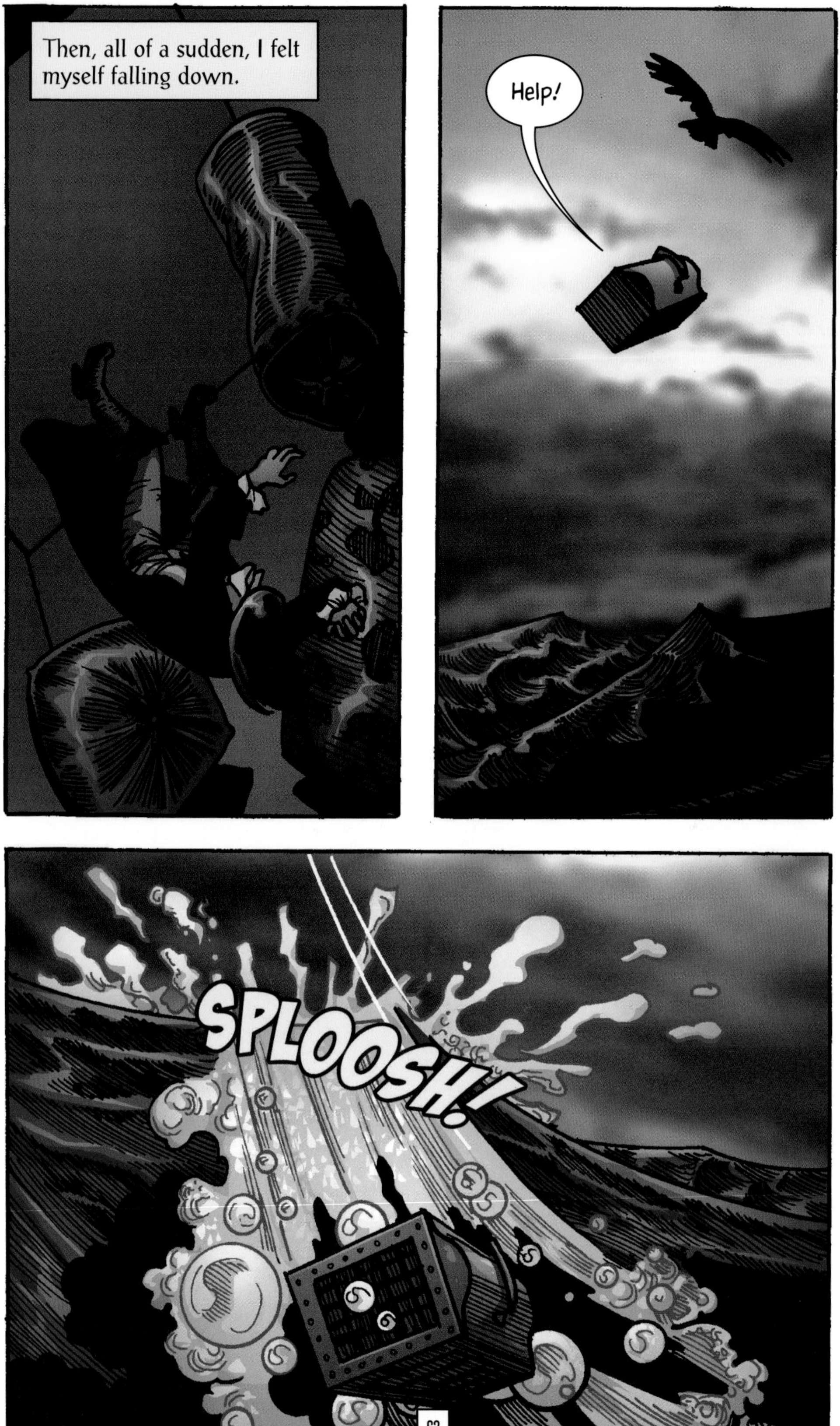
Then, all of a sudden, I felt myself falling down.
Help!
SPLOOSH!

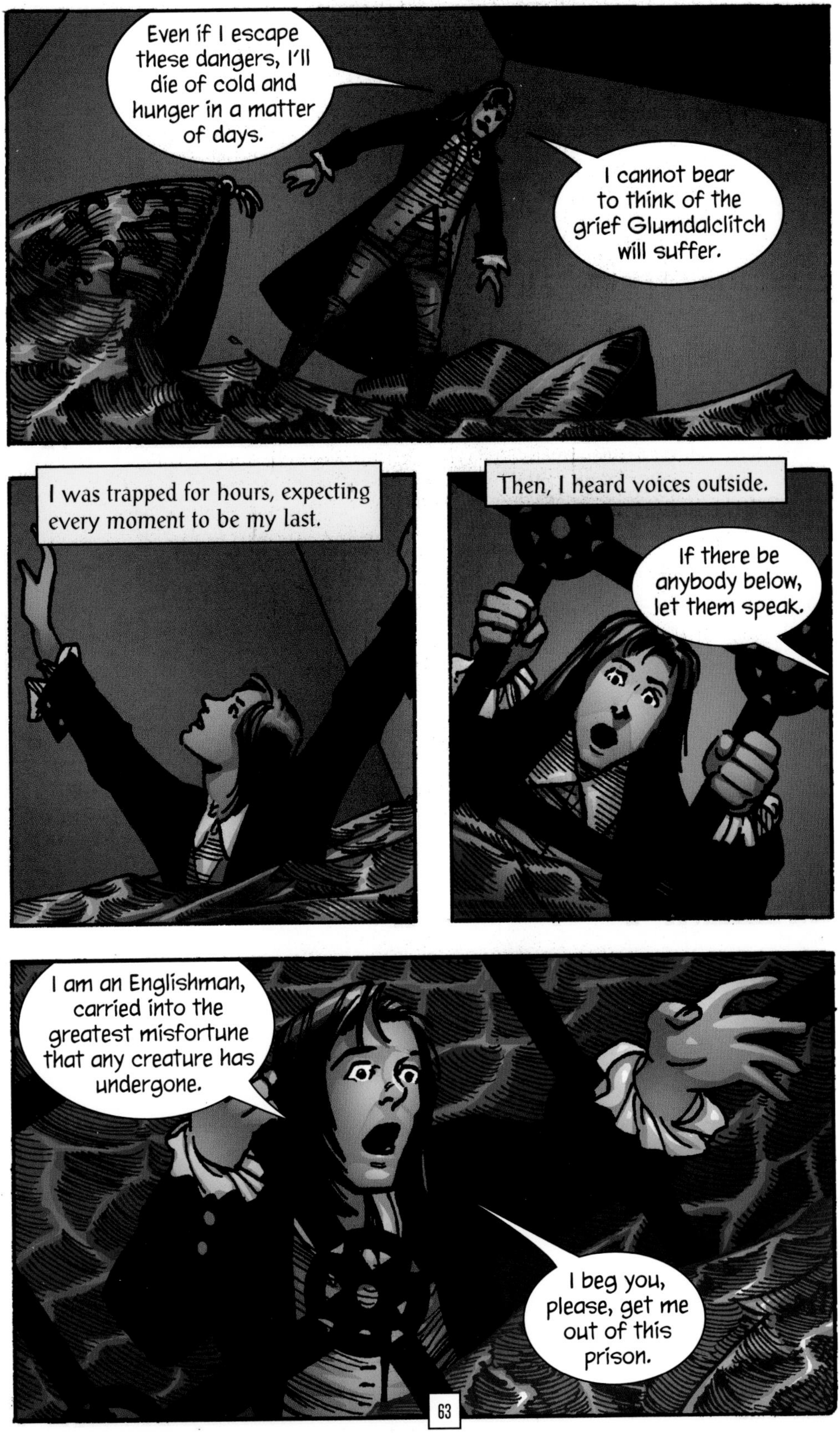
Even if I escape these dangers, I'll die of cold and hunger in a matter of days.
I cannot bear to think of the grief Glumdalclitch will suffer.
I was trapped for hours, expecting every moment to be my last.
Then, I heard voices outside.
If there be anybody below, let them speak.
I am an Englishman, carried into the greatest misfortune that any creature has undergone.
I beg you, please, get me out of this prison.

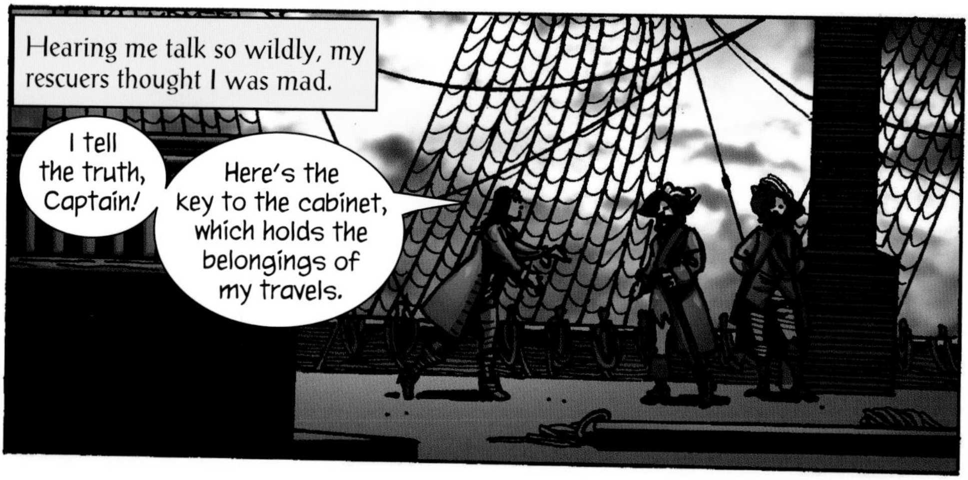
Hearing me talk so wildly, my rescuers thought I was mad.
I tell the truth, Captain!
Here's the key to the cabinet, which holds the belongings of my travels.

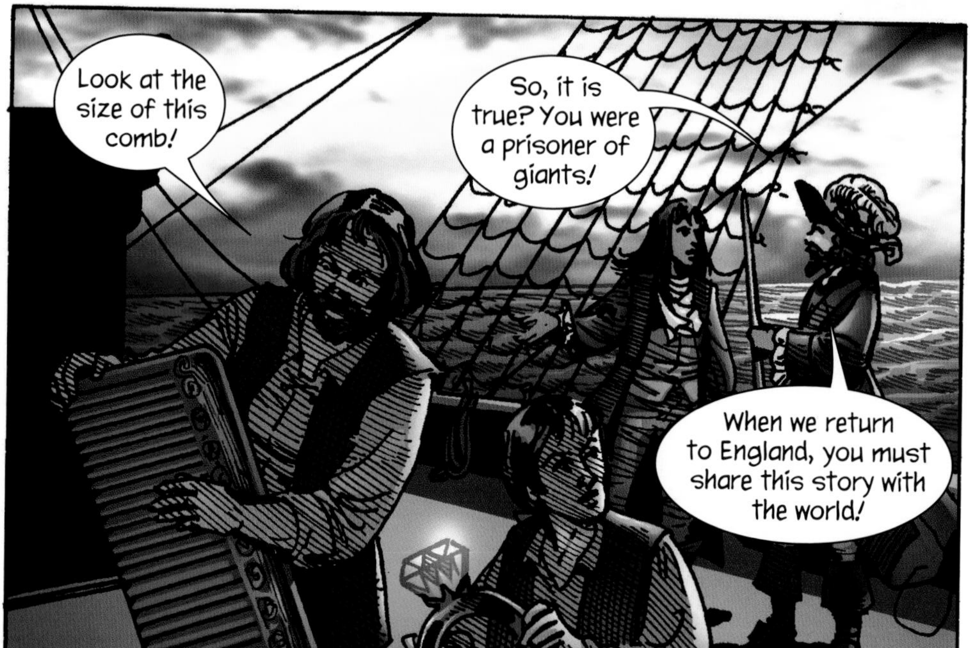
Look at the size of this comb!
So, it is true? You were a prisoner of giants!
When we return to England, you must share this story with the world!

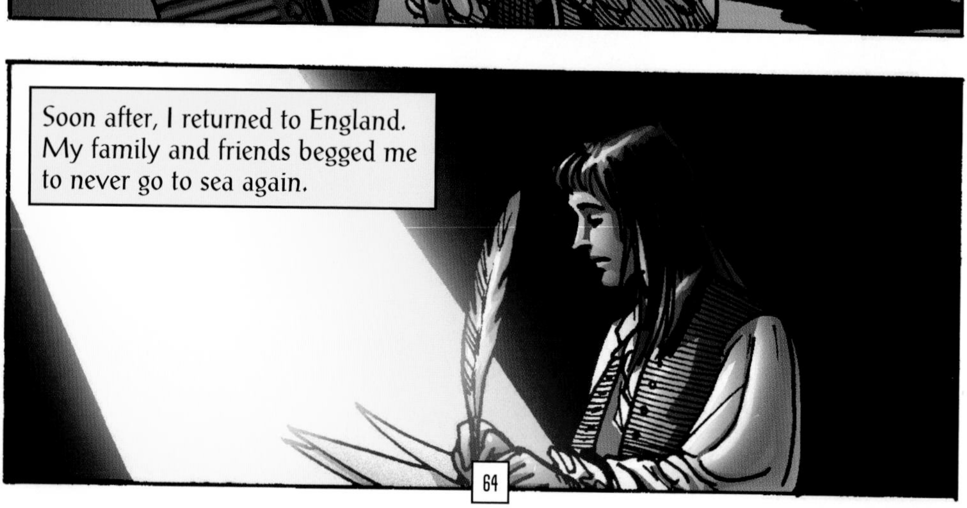
Soon after, I returned to England. My family and friends begged me to never go to sea again.

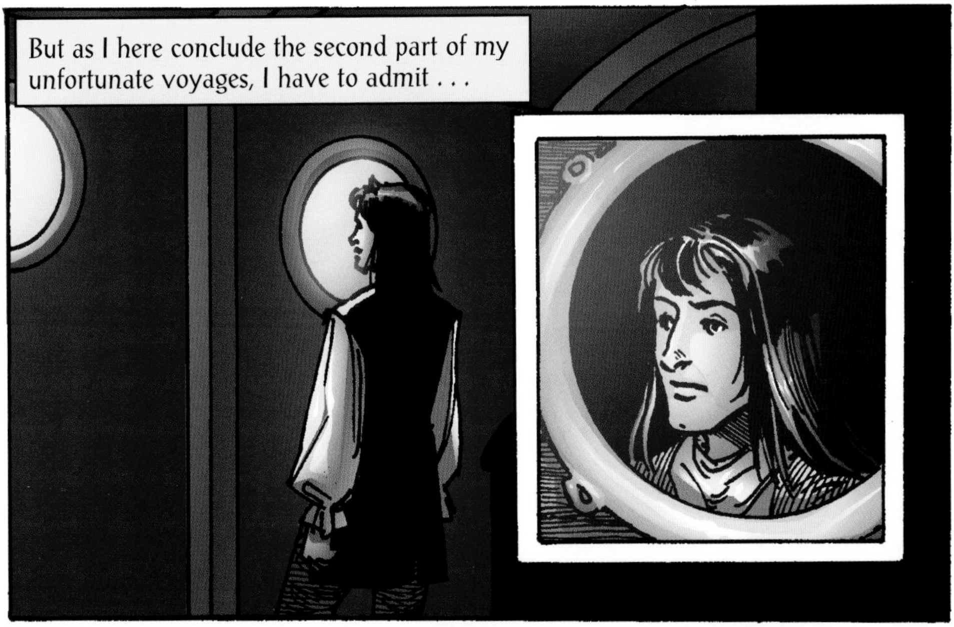
But as I here conclude the second part of my unfortunate voyages, I have to admit . . .

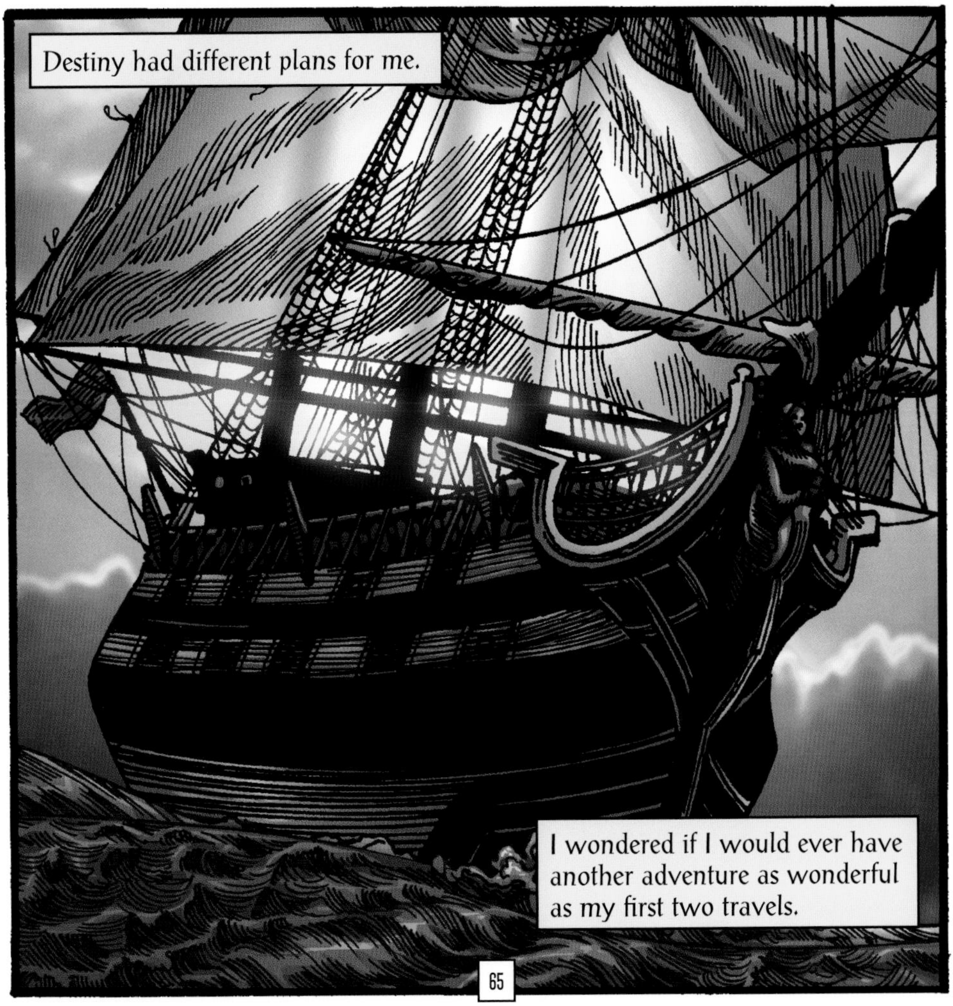
Destiny had different plans for me.
I wondered if I would ever have another adventure as wonderful as my first two travels.

ABOUT THE RETELLING AUTHOR AND ILLUSTRATOR

Growing up in a small Minnesota town, **Donald Lemke** kept himself busy reading comics as well as classic novels. Today, Lemke works as a children's book editor. He recently earned his master's degree in publishing from Hamline University in St. Paul. In his spare time, Lemke has written several graphic novels for kids. This is his first book to combine both his love for comics and classic stories.

Cynthia Martin has worked in comics and animation since 1983. Her credits include Star Wars, Spiderman, and Wonder Woman projects. Martin has also illustrated an extensive series of graphic novels for Capstone Press and two issues of Blue Beetle.

GLOSSARY

capital (KAP-uh-tuhl)—the city where the government is located in a state or country

convict (kuhn-VIKT)—to find proof that someone is guilty of a crime

council (KOUN-suhl)—a group elected to make decisions about a city or country

destiny (DESS-tuh-nee)—the future of your life

emperor (EM-pur-ur)—the male ruler of a country

kingdom (KING-duhm)—an area, usually a country, that has a king and queen as their rulers

liberty (LIB-ur-tee)—freedom from being held prisoner

permission (pur-MISH-uhn)—allowing something to happen

temple (TEM-puhl)—a building used for religious worship

treason (TREE-zuhn)—the crime of going against your own country and helping another country during war

voyage (VOI-ij)—a long journey, often by sea

worships (WUR-shipz)—shows respect to a god

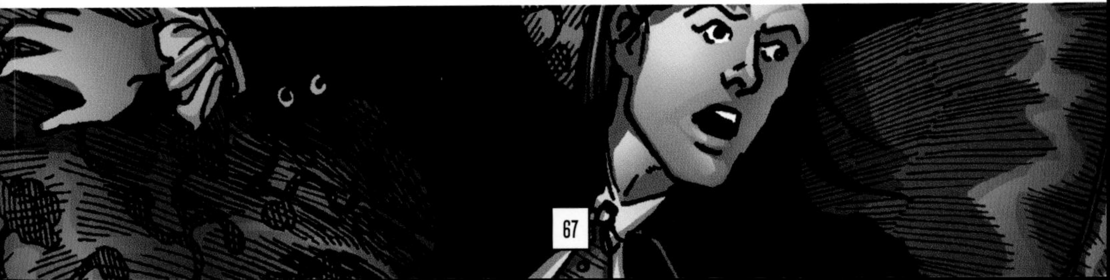

COMMON CORE ALIGNED
READING QUESTIONS

1. There are many different characters in *Gulliver's Travels*. Choose one of these characters and explain how they would narrate some of Gulliver's adventures. What would they say? *("Compare and contrast the point of view from which different stories are narrated.")*

2. True or false: Gulliver enjoys his adventures. Explain your answer using examples from the text and illustrations. *("Refer to details and examples in a text when explaining what the text says explicitly and when drawing inferences from the text.")*

3. What happens to Gulliver when he visits the island of Lilliput? *("Describe in depth a character . . . drawing on specific details in the text.")*

4. Travel is a major theme in this graphic novel. How many places does Gulliver travel to, and what are his experiences at each location? *("Determine a theme of a story.")*

5. The original *Gulliver's Travels* is a novel with no pictures. How do the illustrations in this graphic-novel retelling make the story better? *("Explain major differences between . . . structural elements.")*

COMMON CORE ALIGNED
WRITING QUESTIONS

1. If you were putting on *Gulliver's Travels* as a play and were asked to introduce the audience to Gulliver beforehand, how would you describe him? *("Orient the reader by establishing a situation and introducing a narrator.")*

2. In your opinion, is Gulliver a hero in this story? Why or why not? Write an opinion piece to convince your classmates that you are correct. *("Write opinion pieces on topics or texts, supporting a point of view with reasons and information.")*

3. Write an expository essay that explains and summarizes each of Gulliver's adventures. *("Draw evidence from literary . . . texts to support analysis.")*

4. As you reread *Gulliver's Travels*, keep a journal as if you were Gulliver himself. What would he write about each of his adventures? *("Write routinely over extended time frames.")*

5. Write a letter from Gulliver to his family at home. What would he tell them about his adventures? *("Produce clear and coherent writing in which the development and organization are appropriate to task, purpose, and audience.")*

READ THEM ALL!

JULES VERNE'S
20,000 LEAGUES UNDER THE SEA
A GRAPHIC NOVEL
MARK TWAIN'S
THE ADVENTURES OF TOM SAWYER
A GRAPHIC NOVEL
ANNA SEWELL'S
BLACK BEAUTY
A GRAPHIC NOVEL
VICTOR HUGO'S
THE HUNCHBACK OF NOTRE DAME
A GRAPHIC NOVEL
ROBIN HOOD
A GRAPHIC NOVEL
ROBERT LOUIS STEVENSON'S
TREASURE ISLAND
A GRAPHIC NOVEL
MARY SHELLEY'S
FRANKENSTEIN
A GRAPHIC NOVEL
JULES VERNE'S
JOURNEY TO THE CENTER OF THE EARTH
A GRAPHIC NOVEL
ROBERT LOUIS STEVENSON'S
THE STRANGE CASE OF DR. JEKYLL AND MR. HYDE
A GRAPHIC NOVEL
BY BOWEN & FERRAN
WASHINGTON IRVING'S
THE LEGEND OF SLEEPY HOLLOW
A GRAPHIC NOVEL
BRAM STOKER'S
DRACULA
JONATHAN SWIFT'S
GULLIVER'S TRAVELS
A GRAPHIC NOVEL
ARTHUR CONAN DOYLE'S
THE HOUND OF THE BASKERVILLES
A GRAPHIC NOVEL

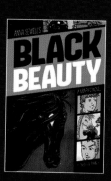

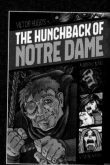

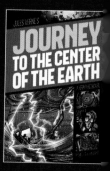

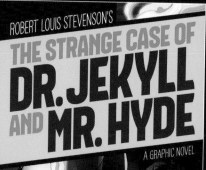

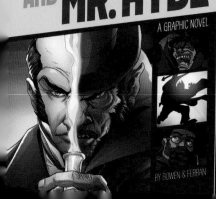

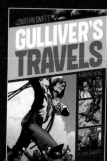

JOHANN DAVID WYSS
THE SWISS FAMILY ROBINSON
A GRAPHIC NOVEL

PERSEUS AND MEDUSA
A GRAPHIC NOVEL

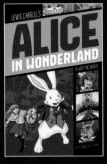

LEWIS CARROLL'S
ALICE
IN WONDERLAND
A GRAPHIC NOVEL

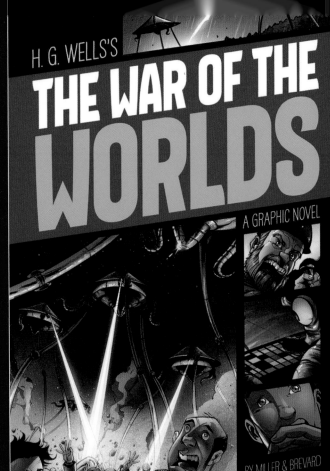

H. G. WELLS'S
THE WAR OF THE WORLDS
A GRAPHIC NOVEL

BY MILLER & BREVARD

H G WELLS'S
THE TIME MACHINE
A GRAPHIC NOVEL

BY DAVIS & TULZ

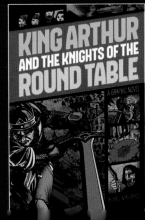

KING ARTHUR
AND THE KNIGHTS OF THE
ROUND TABLE
A GRAPHIC NOVEL

BY HALL & RICHARDS

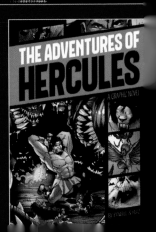

THE ADVENTURES OF
HERCULES
A GRAPHIC NOVEL

BY O'HEARN & NEILL